PIRATES OF MARAUDA

Book 1:
CIRCLES IN TIME

by

FOREST FOX

Cover Art & Illustrations by

Eli D'Elia

FOREST FOX PRESS

Edited by Paul Weisser, PhD
Berkeley, California

Published by Forest Fox Press
Post Office Box 5694
Vallejo, CA 94591

info@forestfoxpress.com
www.forestfoxpress.com

Manufactured in the United States of America
Copyright © 2012 by Forest Fox
All Rights Reserved
ISBN 978-0-9826514-1-4

Any similarity to reality is purely intentional.

This book is dedicated with fond respect and appreciation to all who helped me, too many to list here. You know who you are.

"There was never a time when man was not...." — *Aquarian Gospel*

Prologue

They were the Lamorians, the children of Eden. They were the adventurers of their race, who set out to find the next sweet spot in the Universe, that place in some galaxy on the other side where the cosmic day had just begun. Upon arriving, they would use their marvelous crystal science to create another garden paradise, yet another Eden.

After an epic journey across the stars, the massive space ark encountered a devastating asteroid storm just prior to entering this galaxy. The great ship rolled and dodged as best it could, but it was not meant to be, as all but the saucer section succumbed to the perilous pummeling. The saucer contained an ample amount of their fabulous crystals in a central chamber known as the Middle of the Middle. Never meant to be a lifeboat or shuttle-craft, the saucer was primarily intended to house and protect the Esseen Crystals within its hull of gold repellite. Regarded as the pinnacle of Lamorian engineering and referred to as a time ship because of its ability to go on through the ages unscathed, it was impenetrable except to those original Lamorians who were recognized by the ship's command center.

The saucer containing the children, the medical team, and the sacred crystals smashed its way into the Milky Way, ultimately landing on the Jurassic cauldron that would someday be known as Earth. Oblivious to the perils of their journey, the fragile human cargo awakened from their sleep stasis into a harsh reality.

After many instances of near extinction, the resilient humans found themselves once again on the brink, prisoners inside a massive dormant volcano they called the Wizard's Hat. The Jurassics—raptors, dinosaurs, and monsters of the land, sea, and air—made survival a constant challenge.

The survivors numbered less than a hundred. It was their parents who had been masters of the crystal technology that powered their great starship and so much more. Now these Earthbound children of Mu hardly understood the powers of the Esseen crystals that were stored in their original chamber aboard the saucer and in the pyramid at the center of the Wizard's Hat. The crystals were studied and maintained by the elders, who fervently perused the scattered records of the technology that was their only protection. Nearly the whole population, some ninety-five Atlanteans, as they had come to call themselves, were now within the great hall in the mountain, where they would remain for the duration of the daring attempt they were about to make. The plan was to shift the magnetic poles of the Earth, creating an

Ice Age that would eliminate the Jurassic threat once and for all. The amazing powers of the crystals would do all these things, while the area surrounding the Wizard's Hat would remain stationary in time. Like the center of a wheel, it would remain still as everything moved around it. There were many unknowns in their desperate experiment, but they had no alternative.

I

The five-hour flight from SFO to Oahu never felt short. The days of empty seats and sleeping while stretched out across a whole empty row were long gone. I don't know the reason for this, only that those conditions had not existed in quite a while. I hadn't seen a vacant seat, let alone a whole row, in at least a dozen trips.

This was another of our regular vacations from our dream jobs at Paintball Jungle. My brother Zoe and I wanted to sail to the islands, but our paintball schedule wouldn't allow us the six or seven weeks the trip would require. We were eager to expand our nautical horizons, for after three years of sailing, our longest jaunt was down to the Baja and back. Now we all had Sailing Master certification, and we loved our newest sport and the life at sea. Dad promised that before another year went by, we would take a substantial voyage somewhere, and we were looking forward to it. It had been twenty years now since our paintball odyssey had begun, and our lives had become electrified with the pleasure of playing our favorite sport for a living.

After we landed, rented a Jeep, and checked in at the hotel, our first stop was a visit to our old friends Viri and Miko. We had been visiting the islands for the past seven years, and we had met the brothers on our first visit. We've been close friends ever since.

I'll never forget that July morning, seven years ago. Dad woke up and told Zoe and me that he wanted us to go to Hawaii to learn how to surf. Although the idea came out of nowhere, my brother and I had learned from past experience to take Dad's premonitions and ideas seriously.

One day, twenty years ago now, Dad came home and announced that he would never work on another weekend. Instead, he was going to play as much paintball as he possibly could. The sport was just coming out of its frontier stages back then. One year after Dad's proclamation, he was a top player on a prominent professional team, winning every competition on the circuit. In the three years that followed, he acquired Northern California's premier paintball field, Paintball Jungle, and over $175,000 in tournament prizes. His fifteen consecutive first-place trophies included international competitions in England and France, culminating with a World Championship.

It's been seventeen years since Dad left the pro circuit to be resident pro at the Jungle and captain of the largest recreational team in the world, the San Francisco Hornets, with over four thousand members. Dad's idea of learning to surf was another hit. While not taking on the proportions of professional competition, it has proven to be a very gratifying second sport for us.

Under Miko's expert tutelage, the three of us mastered the skill and have enjoyed seven years of the elation that comes with surfing the big ones. We call Miko and Viri our brothers, and they treat us as family whenever we come to visit.

Originally from Tahiti, they are members of the ancient royal family that ruled those islands before succumbing to colonization. We first met Miko at a Waikiki beachfront surfing school. He was the head instructor and took a special interest in us right from the start. Miko's ranch was always our first stop and where we kept our surfboards when we were away. Viri had a degree in horticulture and worked for the state. Among the brothers' many talents was their production of hand-carved drums and award-winning large-scale models of authentic Tahitian outriggers. The latter, which sold for thousands, were displayed in prominent hotel lobbies all over the world.

When we arrived at the twenty-five-acre estate, the front door of the house was open, as usual. Hailing Miko from the porch, "*Aloha, bradda,*" we entered to find him sipping kava, an herbal drink that dulled the pain from the tattoo he was receiving.

Always dressed in native garb, Miko's body was a work of Tahitian art, displaying the sacred symbolism of his people.

"*Aloha, braddas,* welcome back to our home." Miko's eyes were bleary from his endurance, but, as always, his spirit was soaring.

There were several others sitting around, also dressed traditionally. This was a special day in Miko's life, a holy day, and the mood was reverent but happy. After exchanging greetings, we sat down and the conversation resumed as if we had been there the whole time. Miko lay sprawled out on pillows in the middle of the room, while the artist continued the meticulous task of inscribing the designs and symbols that told the story of the island prince's family lineage, which traced back to the Tahitian gods. This session would complete the sacred tale that now covered eighty percent of his bronze body.

Miko's older brother, Viri, was speaking over the buzz of the tattoo needles. We were soon engrossed in his story about the wreck of the *Sea Lion*, a treasure-laden ship that was believed to have gone down in heavy seas off the Kona Coast late in the nineteenth century.

"There have been countless attempts to locate her last resting place, but no one has ever found a trace," Viri said. He went on to tell how the *Sea Lion*, a known leper transport, was taking patients from Tahiti to the colony on Molokai. "Her real mission was to smuggle a fortune in gold and precious stones from China to the Big Island." Viri pointed out that the current sea laws made searching for the prize almost worthless. "If the *Sea Lion* were discovered, the finder would receive a very small fraction of its true value. First of all, any artifacts found would automatically be consigned to a museum, while any gold, diamonds, or other valuables would be federal property."

After he somberly described the sea search laws, Viri's eyes began to twinkle as a sly smile exposed his pearly whites, and he continued, "These laws have eliminated the incentive for searching, and now there is little, if any, chance that anyone will ever find her...that is, before *we* do."

The tales of the *Sea Lion* were always a favorite subject of conversation for Viri and Miko. The brothers had their own theory for why the treasure was never found.

"We believe," said Viri, "the *Sea Lion* sank somewhere between Molokai and Maui. The stories of her sinking off the Kona Coast were meant to keep everyone away from the true location." The brothers were convinced this was the case.

"The Gazetteer records for that period," Viri continued, "report the typhoon that sank the *Sea Lion* was of such magnitude that any ship caught in that storm never could have made it past the straits of Lanai." Viri was adamant about this premise. In the past ten years, he and his brother had led four expensive searches between Molokai and Lahaina, but to no avail. "It's down there somewhere. We'll find it sooner or later, I'm sure of it."

Dad was always enthralled with their stories about the *Sea Lion.* The only part of their stories we hadn't heard before was about the sea search laws. When Viri declared his certainty of eventually finding the prize, Dad asked, "What about the problems with the search laws?"

Viri's eyes squinted slightly as he responded, "*Bradda,* when we get our hands on the prize, we have ways around that obstacle, believe me."

Everyone laughed as Viri finished talking about his magnificent obsession, and Miko stood up and displayed his.

As the afternoon concluded, more of Miko's friends joined

the gathering. Out in the backyard, the *kalua* pork baked slowly in the *imu*, an underground oven. The whole pig was packed with hot stones and *lau lau* leaves filled with a variety of sumptuous fare, including fish, chicken, *poi*, sweet potatoes, breadfruit, and bananas. The alluring aroma of these delicacies had everyone gravitating toward their promise, while pulsating drums and chants announced the beginning of the *luau*. Served in hollowed coconut shells, the savory repast had a soulful flare.

The sun began its descent from the cloudless sapphire, curtailing another euphoric day as the gentle trades swirled the intoxicating scents and sounds of these children of paradise celebrating their fate. Our acquaintance with Miko and his family gave us an insider's experience of the timeless harmony of these islands. As the setting sun seared the horizon with its crimson influence, the sound of the conch and a traditional *hula* started the evening's entertainment.

Among the three exotic dancers was Viri and Miko's younger sister, Leia. Her captivating sensuality personified a divine image of the essence of Polynesia. Her *ti* leaf skirt swayed to the music, while the fluidity of her hands and hips told the stories of her people in hypnotic movements.

The hula dancing gave way to the intense rhythms of the large *pahu* drums as fire dancers in *malo* loincloths tossed spinning, double-tipped flaming torches high into the darkness. Next came a chorus of *Kumulipo* chants, whose exotic harmonies told of the pantheon of gods and the creation of humankind.

The feasting never stopped. Miko's grandmother, the family

kupuna, stood up to tell stories about the *Menehune*, the little people of Hawaii who shunned humans and possessed magical powers. Stone walls completed in a single night were attributed to them. The *kupuna* sang a sacred chant. Her ageless voice enthralled us as she told of the first Hawaiians, who came from the Marquesas in great double-hulled canoes. With words that seemed to float on the evening's gentle breezes, she described how their savage fierceness was quelled by the island's spirit of *aloha*.

Next, as Viri sang and played his ukulele, we all laughed at his songs about his adventures with his favorite *wahines*. Everyone joined in when the chorus sang a favorite song from World War II called "You Can't Conquer Niihau, No How." Before we knew it, another day had begun, and people started heading home.

Miko invited us to join him at Waimea Bay in the morning. "There's a forecast for big surf tomorrow," he said. "We'll hang a few for old time's sake."

We readily agreed to meet him and, thanking him for the unforgettable day and night, took our leave.

Back at the hotel, Zoe recapped what we now knew about the *Sea Lion*: "Viri was adamant about where she went down. You'd think after four expeditions, they might consider other possibilities."

Shaking his head, Dad said, "That stretch between Lahaina and Molokini is a pretty long expanse. They could probably triple their efforts and still miss it. Luck will play a major part if they're to be successful."

"One thing's for sure," I said, "the *Sea Lion* didn't go down near Molokini. If she did, she would have been found by now. That place is visited by hundreds of divers and snorkelers every day. The last time we were there, there must have been twenty excursion boats tied up, and that's been going on for years."

When everyone agreed on that point, the subject changed to speculation about the morning surf.

"Miko expects big waves," Zoe said. "He wouldn't be going otherwise."

Again, we agreed with Zoe's summation and drifted off to sleep with visions of water giants in our heads.

Zoe was up bright and early. By the time Dad and I were up and about, he had waxed all three surfboards. Arriving on the north shore, we found conditions on Waimea Bay ideal, with a moderate offshore fetch lifting the swells to ten- and fifteen-foot curls. These waves were formidable precursors to the thirty- to fifty-foot winter surf that Waimea is famous for. We found Viri and his friend Miki Aikau, a legendary boardsman, waiting for us on the beach.

"*Aloha, braddas*," Viri called. "You remember Miki, don't you?"

Miki smiled warmly as we renewed our acquaintance from the previous year. Miko and some others were waving to us from their boards beyond the white water. Wasting no time, we all started out toward the fun. Dad, Zoe, and I were spared the usual *haole* stigma that can dampen a mainlander's fun. The company we were keeping expunged any doubt about us in the eyes of the local soul surfers, and the *aloha* flowed freely among us.

We were halfway out to the break when Miko and another surfer took off on a fifteen-foot monster. Planing down the face and pumping for maximum speed, they cut back in the direction the wave was breaking in an effort to get into the pocket. As the curl began its plunge into the trough below, Miko's efforts got him barreled within the tube of white water. With one hand trailing, he sped along on his achievement.

Miko's friend, a fraction too late, was caught by the deluge, sending him over the falls and out of sight. The anxious moments that followed seemed much longer as we scanned the white water for any sign of him. Tension was mounting when he popped out above the foamy brine and gave a wave that all was well.

Refocusing on our destination, we just had time to duck dive, pushing our boards underwater, nose first, through an oncoming wave that would have gotten us off to a bad start. Miko and his buddy waved to us as we surveyed the perfect swells from the shoulder.

Viri was next to take off, aiming toward the curl. Performing a classic floater, he took a "goofy foot" stance with his left foot on the back of the board, executing a perfect cutback. Riding up on top of the breaking wave, he proceeded to walk to the front of his board and "hang ten"—ten toes over the nose—as everyone in the water and on the beach cheered him on.

Miko and his friend snaked over to me. "Rob," Miko said, "this is my *bradda* Eli from California. He's fearless. He was my star student seven years ago, and he's still the quickest study I've ever had. Eli, meet Rob Hanakele."

I knew who Rob was, although I'd never met him. As the World Champion reached over to shake my hand, I flushed a bit from Miko's introduction.

"Glad to meet you, *bradda*," Rob said, "let's see something."

I smiled. "*Aloha*," I said. "I know who you are, and it's an honor to meet you. I doubt I'll show you anything, but here goes."

After being challenged by Rob Hanakele, I had no choice but to try to execute Miko's latest lesson. Miko first demonstrated the "aerial maneuver" to me on our last visit to the islands. The trick had been my main focus ever since. Inspired by snowboarders, pro surfers everywhere have developed their version by going airborne and successfully returning to the same wave. Easier said than done. So far, I had been successful in about half of my attempts.

Choosing an appropriate swell, I took off down the face just ahead of the curl. Pumping for speed and cutting back toward the curl with an abrupt snap off the lip, I was airborne and rotating back around into the wave as the pipeline formed over me, and away I went.

What a day! I could do no wrong. Each wave was better than the last as the board responded to my every whim. Dad and Zoe were also enjoying a flawless day as they negotiated wave after wave with great satisfaction.

When I started to tire, I wouldn't admit it to myself, wanting this day to never end. Dad had already announced that he was taking a break, so he was watching now from the beach as I maneuvered into position to meet what looked like the biggest wave of the day. There were no fewer than a dozen of us waiting in rapt anticipation when the mammoth swell started to peak. In the last instant, another surfer snaked behind me, cutting off my ideal position, a move regarded by everyone as bad etiquette. In essence, he was stealing my wave out from under me.

It was too late to do anything about it. We both took off, streaking down the face of the water giant as its curl blocked the sun. Dropping into my path, he was cutting me off once again. Pumping in an effort to avoid a collision, I was forced to fade before making a hasty cutback toward the curl. The maneuver took me into the ensuing deluge. Pitched off my board, over the falls I went, slammed to the bottom of the reef by the merciless inundation of white water known as the "wash cycle." It sucked me off the bottom and tumbled me over and over again. I remember thinking this was it. I was out of air and didn't know which way was up, even if I could have escaped the relentless suction. That was when I was whacked on the head by what must have been my own board, and the lights went out.

"Hang in there, *bradda*, I'll have you on the beach in a few minutes." Miko's words sounded distant, familiar, and meaningless. He was guiding me back toward shore with his big toe on my board while paddling from his. I was semi-conscious. It was like a dream. "Talk to me, *bradda*, are you alright?"

I responded half-heartedly, "Yeah, what happened?"

"You'll be okay. I'll have you on the beach in no time."

Oblivious to what had happened, I lay dazed and limp on my board as we cut across the white water between the swells and the beach. Scudding along with my Tahitian brother, I was in a dream state as myriad images of last night's *luau*, music, fire dancers, sinking ships, and Molokini produced a synesthesia of feeling from the essence and timelessness of these islands and the surf beneath this ultramarine arch of heaven.

Dad had watched the whole ordeal from the shore. I knew by the grave look on his face that he was distressed as Miko helped me from my board to the beach.

"He's okay," Miko said. "Bumped his head, that's all."

Miko's words soothed Dad's anxiety as he examined the egg-sized lump on my head. "Man, that was one big wave. I thought you'd bought it that time. Who was that dude who burned you like that?"

I didn't respond as I lay down on the blanket, so the subject was dropped.

Leaning over me, Dad peered into my eyes. "No dilation...I guess you're okay."

Zoe never knew I was in trouble. He had caught the wave that followed mine and ridden the tube almost a quarter-mile down the shoreline. Then he continued surfing with Miko and the others. While Dad sat beside me under the umbrella, I fell into a deep sleep.

When I awoke, the sun was an hour from setting. Dad looked

at me, still concerned. "You had quite a little nap. How do you feel?"

Not yet focused, I was preoccupied with my dreams. "I saw where the *Sea Lion* went down," I said. "Viri was right. It's between Maui and Kahoolawe near Molokini."

My dream evaporated as I regained consciousness, but not before Dad had taken note of my reverie. *"That's* interesting! Saw it all in your dream, did you? I wonder if you're onto something."

Zoe chimed in, "It wouldn't be the first time Eli has led us into our destiny. If he hadn't asked for a paintball gun that Christmas, twenty years ago, who knows *where* we would be today."

Miko also heard the account of my sleeping vision. "I have business to attend to tomorrow," he said. "But you're welcome to take my boat if you wanna go over and check it out."

Dad needed little encouragement. As an ex-Navy frogman, with a great passion for diving, he had been hoping to get some scuba diving in on this trip. Miko's offer was all he needed to sketch out a two- or three-day expedition then and there.

It was another in the seemingly endless chain of perfect days in these paradisiacal islands as we caught the 7 A.M. flight over to Maui. At the Lahaina marina, we picked up Miko's boat, the *Honu-luau.* The classic thirty-five-foot yawl had a mainsail and a forward jib. It was very similar to our own *Sea Major*, not only in size and rigging but also in its excellent maneuverability. Miko told us that *Honu-luau* meant "sea turtle."

After renting the necessary scuba gear, we sailed up along Maui's south coast to Molokini. As the setting sun set the evening sky ablaze, we dropped anchor behind the crater of the ancient submerged volcano peeking above the waves.

"You said it went down between Maui and Kahoolawe near Molokini, right?" Dad asked.

It was no use; we went over and over those moments when I awoke, spouting about yesterday's phantasm.

"At this point, Dad, you remember more about my dream than I do," I said.

There wasn't much to it, but Dad and Zoe both remembered me saying it was near Molokini.

Dad continued, "Well, if it's near Molokini, it must be on the Kahoolawe side. Otherwise, it would have certainly been found by one of the countless daily visitors to the crater."

"On that we can all agree," Zoe said, "so let's start looking right here in the morning and work our way toward the little island. Maybe we'll get lucky."

Basing our diving plan on Zoe's summation, we spent the rest of the evening sprawled out on the deck stargazing, as the gentle rocking took us off to dreamland.

Blocked by the mountain, the sun rises late on the south side of Maui. By the time it appeared over the island's high country, everything was ready for our first dive of the day. As distant thunderheads made hollow threats to the ultramarine firmament,

I couldn't help thinking they were a metaphor for our intentions and aspirations.

"We've got about as much chance of finding the *Sea Lion*," I said, "as those thunderheads do of darkening this day."

Dad was more upbeat: "Maybe so, or maybe we'll get lucky. Whichever it is, I'm sure beautiful things await our efforts, so let's be off."

With that, Dad fell backward over the side, and we followed. The sea floor was ten fathoms below. Shafts of golden sunlight illuminated the coral and sea life, which was in emerald abundance. Not far from our point of origin, there was a ledge that dropped off into the shadows.

Dad led the way down into a maze of coral canyons as we began snapping pictures of the august formations and their silent tenants. Beneath us, an easy moving stingray left dust clouds over the sandy bottom as he patrolled his domain. Fifteen minutes into the dive found us completely enthralled with our environment.

Spotting something, Zoe abruptly dove toward the sea floor to recover it from in-between the jagged formations.

At first, I thought he had retrieved a broken piece of coral as he swam back toward us, stopping in the glow of one of the shafts of sunlight. It became obvious from his gesticulations that he was excited about whatever he had retrieved.

When Dad and I swam over to him, Zoe's eyes were pushing his eyebrows above the seal of his diving mask as he held his prize up in the light. At first, it appeared to be a piece of coral, but as we focused we realized that it was a ship's bell encrusted with coral. After a closer examination, Dad signaled us to surface.

As we popped our heads out of the water, Dad was already talking to us: "Zoe, you stay here while Eli and I get the boat. Man, it looks like you've found something there. Hold onto it, we'll be back in a flash."

It was a hundred yards to the boat. As we swam, I noticed there was a change in the wind and that the mood of what had been another perfect day in paradise was changing.

Zoe treaded water the whole time, until we dropped anchor over the new site. When he came aboard, we got our first good look at his prize.

"Look at this!" Zoe said, pointing at an exposed spot at the base of the middling sized ship's bell. "That's definitely an *S* engraved there. The coral somehow missed covering it. Look here."

Zoe still had his scuba gear on as he pointed out the distinguishable letter amidst the crustaceans. A streak of lightning cracked across the encroaching thunderheads, but Zoe took little notice.

"I'm sure we're on the trail of the *Sea Lion!*" he said.

By midday, there was intermittent lightning and thunderclaps, but we carried on with our preparations for another dive. Eager to continue the search, over the side we went into a darker but still negotiable environment. The lack of direct sunlight hampered our progress at first, until we adjusted to the different shades of grey. After two more hours and as many dives, we found nothing new.

During a long break on deck, we examined the relic, passing it back and forth many times while sharing day-old sandwiches and bottled water. Zoe started chipping away at the encrustation despite Dad's concern about damaging any clues that might be revealed when we got the bell to shore. Once there, we would submerge it in a chemical bath that would dissolve the coral's effect.

"I'll just give it a few whacks," Zoe said. "Maybe there's something more here."

He chipped away at it with a jackknife as the sky continued to darken. We were preparing the diving gear when Zoe plucked us from our focus with a shrill hoot.

"Whoa! Man, check this out!"

We scrambled over to see what had recharged his enthusiasm.

"Look at this!" he said, holding up the bell.

His chipping had revealed the letters *L* and *I*, which were proportionately spaced from the *S*, suggesting the distinct possibility that these letters were indeed part of the words *Sea Lion*.

As Zoe's elation ignited our own, the blackening sky exploded with a torrential downpour, sending us scampering below deck, where we were snug with our prize behind a battened hatch and consumed with plans for our next dive.

"It's getting too late for another dive today," Dad said. "Let's wait for morning and the sunlight. We'll need all the help we can get. Chances are the trail will lead to deeper water."

Dad's speculations didn't dampen our hopes, even though Zoe and I knew we were already at our limit, since we had never gone deeper than a hundred and fifty feet. Dad was a different story. The skies cleared just as the sun was setting. Before its crimson bands faded into the sable mantle, Dad reminded us of what all sailors know: red sky at night, sailor's delight.

Sleep wasn't a problem; the *Honu-luau* rocked us gently through the night.

The morning was another pristine example of paradise as the great fireball ascended toward its zenith in the flawless blue vault of heaven. Zoe and I were impatient to resume the search for the *Sea Lion*. We waited while Dad fitted his air supply with a device that would prevent it from becoming poisonous if he exceeded three hundred feet. Our plan was to continue to scour the area from yesterday's find toward Kahoolawe. It was obvious that the depths in that direction were steadily increasing. Our limited diving experience wouldn't allow us to probe deeper, but Dad was now equipped to do so if necessary.

"If it's down there, we'll find it," he said while he harnessed the ninety-five-pound rig to his back and sat on the bulwark.

Once he was under water, the cumbersome air supply would weigh less than twenty-five pounds, affording him a wide range of operation.

"Okay, let's go," Dad said. Then, fitting his mouthpiece, he fell back into the sea.

We were twenty minutes into the dive having exceeded one

hundred and seventy-five feet, when Dad signaled us not to go any deeper, for the sea floor was continuing its downward slope. As he descended, we watched him from above. He was almost out of sight when he suddenly came swimming back toward us, carrying something. To our surprise, he continued his ascent past us.

We followed him to where the shafts of sunlight still illuminated the emerald brine. As he held up his coral-covered find to the light, there was no mistaking what it was. Although three sides were encrusted, the side that rested on the seabed was coral-free.

Gold! It was a gold bar—there could be no mistake.

Once again, Dad signaled us to the surface, where he waited while we moved the boat over to him.

Back on board and hovering over the sight of our find, we were beside ourselves with this latest discovery. Engraved on the exposed side of the golden bar was a Chinese symbol, reassuring us that we were indeed on the trail of the *Sea Lion*.

Although Dad had noticed that the current increased the deeper he went, he was undaunted: "It's getting pretty deep down there. I'll take the camera along and continue the search alone while you two stay on board."

Zoe didn't like the idea of waiting on the surface, but there was no alternative, so he reluctantly agreed to Dad's instructions.

"Don't be down there all day," he said.

Dad smiled back. "Only as long as it takes to find what we're looking for."

He gave us the thumbs up and, falling back into the water, disappeared.

To distract himself, Zoe started talking about how much he enjoyed sailing the *Honu-luau*, the *Sea Turtle*. "Man," he said, "we've got to take the *Sea Major* on an extended cruise. I love this feeling of life at sea. There's a whole sense of adventure out here. It's not that I don't love the world of paintball. It's just that I can feel the sea beckoning us to a life of treasure hunting and adventures without any deadlines. It would be a whole new way of experiencing time itself."

I had to admit he was speaking for both of us: "Yeah, I'm with you, brother, but we have to talk Dad into it. He always says that business comes first, and everything else comes second."

Zoe nodded and began putting our gear in order. Trying not to notice the time, we occupied ourselves with making everything shipshape and ready for whatever was next. After nearly two hours, there was still no sign of the diving expert. While the afternoon trade winds whipped the placid Pacific swells into feisty little whitecaps, we were becoming more anxious with each passing minute. Even with three air tanks and conservative breathing tactics, there would hardly be enough air to last this long.

"Man, it's getting late!" Zoe muttered. "Why does he have to cut it this close?"

Trying to keep the anxiety to a minimum, I answered Zoe's

rhetorical question: "Don't worry, he'll be along any minute now."

As I said this, relief came bursting through the whitecaps fifty yards off our starboard bow, waving his camera at us.

"There he is!" Zoe yelled. "Let's go!"

In the time it took for me to hoist the mainsail, Zoe had the anchor on board. As we came alongside Dad, Zoe scooped him into the boat. Dad handed him the camera and slipped out of his harness while I dropped the sail once again and then the anchor. Dad was beaming.

As Zoe's anxiety changed to relief, he gazed at Dad. "What took you so long?"

"Take a look."

Zoe switched modes on the camera and studied the tiny screen. "You found it! Eli, look, he found the *Sea Lion!*"

Looking over his shoulder, I was able to see that the grey images did indeed look like a sunken hull. Clicking back, I saw that the third image was of its stern. The words *Sea Lion* were still quite legible.

"Oh, man, what do we do now?" Zoe asked as he continued to click through the short sequence. "Miko's gonna flip out when he sees *this*."

By now Dad had caught his breath. "First thing we do is rig a cargo net I can take back down there. There are chests of gold and all sorts of loot spread out on the bottom from when she broke apart. By the looks of things, I figure she must have cracked open after hitting the crater. Before we leave, I wanna take one chest back with us, but right now mark this spot on the chart."

We were spinning with excitement, but Dad had his wits about him, directing us with the priorities of the moment.

After rigging the remaining air tanks with his breathing device, Dad was back in the water with a four-hundred-foot rope and small cargo net in tow.

"It won't take me long to reach bottom," he said. "When you feel a double tug on the line, that'll be the signal to hoist away."

It felt much longer than the twenty minutes or so that actually passed before we felt the double tug. The line was quite heavy, but our adrenaline compensated. We had the catch on deck by the time Dad climbed aboard.

The first thing he said after looking around was, "Get it stowed below, before anyone sees what we've got here."

Zoe and I looked at each other and then in all directions, but there were neither ships nor sailors anywhere in sight.

Noticing our quizzical expressions, Dad explained, "Never mind, we can't be too careful now. There's millions strewn about down there, and it will attract people like a magnet if we aren't especially careful about our every move from now on."

The magnitude of our discovery was just starting to sink in as we looked all around again before stashing the chest below deck. We passed the evening gazing at the five gold bars and planning our next move. We decided to up anchor in the morning and head directly for Miko's ranch with the news. Before leaving the area, however, we would make a brief stop on the crater side of Molokini to load the camera with images of the myriad sea life that congregated there, so as to bury our pictures of the *Sea Lion* deep within the camera's one-gig chip.

Sleep came late, if at all, for our excitement kept slumber at bay. After the brief stop at Molokini, we set sail for Honolulu.

"We should be there before sunset," Dad said as he trimmed the jib. "When we dock at Waikiki, you two can go and get Miko while I stand watch."

As we scudded along before the wind, with Maui off our stern, Zoe started in on Dad: "This find changes everything. With our share of the prize, we can take that extended cruise we've been talking about. We can get a gazetteer and start looking for more treasure, or maybe sail to Africa and back. I don't care where we go...I just wanna log in some sea adventures. I'm really enjoying sailing the *Sea Turtle*. It makes me want more than ever to take our boat to some exotic places. But first, let's sail to Martha's Vineyard to visit Shanda, and tell her what we've found. What do you say, Dad?"

He looked at me and smiled. "Remember, boys, we can't tell *anyone* about this, not even your sister." Then, turning to Zoe, he said, "Keep her on the numbers, mate."

Zoe glanced at the ship's compass and adjusted the helm. "C'mon, Dad, what do you think about taking the *Sea Major* on a real cruise somewhere?"

Taking a seat next to Zoe, he answered, "I'd say you've got the sea raging in your blood, and you won't be happy till you answer its call. However, we haven't landed this goldfish yet, and we have a big season planned for the Jungle next year. There's the Young Guns Tournament Series and the One-on-One Classic, not to mention the multitude of corporate events already scheduled. Let's just see how all this plays out before we make any more plans."

Zoe wasn't happy with Dad's answer. "Whatever," he said. "All I know is that I've got a big trip swelling up inside of me, and it won't be too much longer before I'll have to do something about it. Besides, Brett and the crew can handle all the action the Jungle has booked for the next ten years, if necessary."

The conversation was over for the moment. Dad got up and walked toward the bow, saying, "We'll see, son, we'll see. First things first."

Back on the island, Miko studied the pictures intently and, beaming, he handed the camera to his brother. Viri gave out with the Tahitian version of a howling "Yippee-kai-yay!"

Miko was quick to hush his brother's exuberance: "Quiet, Viri! No one must know what we have found!"

When a few members of his family came from different parts of the house to see what the excitement was all about, Miko pretended to be describing my surfing skills to Viri.

"You should've seen him! It was the longest ride in the tube I've ever seen."

Viri played along with the conversation, and eventually the family members resumed whatever they had been doing.

Soon we were back on board the *Honu-luau* with Dad and all

that gold. Miko explained what must happen next if we were to bypass the vulturous grasp of the government.

"First of all, I'll contact my uncle on the Big Island. He has a network that can digest everything we can recover for the best return. Tomorrow we'll sail over to Kona, where he'll be waiting with cash for what you have here. Next, we'll return to Molokini and start doing what must be done."

Dad told Miko and Viri that from what he could see, there was a considerable amount of treasure to be collected.

"There's a large breech in the side of the hull," he told them. "This chest was just outside of it, along with many others, including some that were broken open."

Miko nodded. "If the records are accurate, there should be *millions* in gold and precious stones in that wreckage. We won't be able to retrieve it all in one trip. It'll probably take many visits to recover everything, and that must be done skillfully so as not to attract any attention."

"We would never have found the treasure without you, Miko," Dad said. "We'll be happy with anything you want to share with us, but we'll leave the recovery operations to you. We have very little time left before we must return home to our business."

"We'll handle everything," Miko said. "Your cut will most certainly exceed two million dollars when all is said and done."

Two days later, we were docked at the marina in Kona, where Miko's Uncle Gil met us. He was a portly Hawaiian, full of the *aloha* spirit. Meeting him was like meeting a great chief. It was obvious that Miko was very fond of him. He invited us to his home, where we were warmly welcomed by his whole family.

That evening, there was another *luau* attended by relatives and friends. After the fire dancers performed, Uncle Gil took us into his office and explained that while a 400-ounce bar is worth $156,000, after everyone involved was considered, our end would be $40,000 per bar. Then he presented us with $200,000 in crisp hundred dollar bills.

"This is your cut of what we hope will be many times more when everything is recovered."

Of course, we were delighted with the arrangement and thanked our gracious partners profusely.

By noon the next day, we were on a flight back to California. On the plane, Zoe pitched the idea of an extended cruise a few more times to Dad. As usual, this technique of Zoe's never failed to chip away at Dad's resistance.

II

Nearly a year had passed since our Hawaiian adventure with Miko. The joint venture with our Tahitian brothers continued to yield gracious allotments that far exceeded our modest anticipations. According to Miko, there was still no end in sight. After relentless pestering on Zoe's part, we finally embarked on the *Sea Major* for an extended cruise down to Panama and through the canal to the Atlantic to explore the recently altered area of the Bermuda Triangle. A massive earthquake had left a vast new sea cliff in the infamous zone of legend and mystique.

At its epicenter, the undersea quake measured 7.4 and sent killer *tsunamis* around the globe. Responding to reports of the new sea cliff formed two hundred miles off the Bermuda coast, we were over the site exactly one month after the seismic event. Countless species of fish swam along with us as we explored the area. There was a vivid contrast: on one side, the sun shot gold and amber shafts through the aquamarine to the sandy sea floor;

on the other, a foreboding blackness swelled out from the newly formed abyss.

After waiting for a solid wall of golden fish to pass, we were about to continue with our search when a vivid feeling of sheer benevolence surged through me in a flush of joy. I was at a complete loss to understand this sudden dazzling wave of emotion, and wondered if my brother were sharing my experience. Then we saw it. Amazement, excitement, and adrenaline can make it hard to breathe. The spectacle beneath us kept us focused as we regained our respiratory rhythm. We had found treasure before, but this was unbelievable. Even as I realized what I was looking at, I found myself trying to explain it away. It was stunningly highlighted on the edge of the shelf, shimmering in the golden green light.

There was no mistaking what we were looking at—a saucer! It was big, real big, a craft from somewhere lying beneath us in two hundred feet of water.

Time was running out, so I snapped a couple of pictures, signaled Zoe, and we headed for the surface. When we came up, yelling about what we had found, we startled Dad. The boat was bobbing now as the seas started to show signs of a change. Seeing Dad's expression as he watched the way we were swimming toward the boat, I could tell that he thought a shark was after us.

"Eli, what *is* it?"

"Dad, get the camera and suit up!"

Responding to the rising chop, the boat leaned, almost catching Dad off balance, as we scrambled aboard.

Compensating adroitly and relieved there was no shark, he asked, "What've you got?"

Ignoring the question, Zoe yelled, "We need fresh tanks!"

The three of us were in a frenzy as we changed tanks. Dad was following orders, but not getting answers. What transpired within a minute seemed like an hour to Dad as he repeated his demand: "Tell me what you found! You want us to leave the *Sea Major* unattended? For *what*?"

Finally looking Dad in the eyes, Zoe said, "Some kind of craft..., a flying saucer..., I don't know. Let's go!"

Slipping into his gear, Dad looked at me. It still wasn't sinking in.

"I don't know what we saw," I said, "so let's get back down there. I'm telling you, Dad, you're gonna flip out when you see this!"

"We don't have much time," he said. "There's a storm coming."

But Dad's weather warning went unheeded. Normally, when a squall was coming, we headed for safe harbor. Not only was that not an option this far out, but I doubt we would have left anyway. We were too excited.

"Let's go!" Dad said, grabbing his camera and falling backward into the sea.

Soon we were hovering over the site of the strange craft. Just as before, I felt a warm, gracious feeling of emotion as Zoe looked over at me with raised eyebrows and a quizzical gaze, indicating his similar experience.

Animated now, Dad was swimming around, trying to take it all in with the camera. Two hundred feet is deeper than Zoe and I had ever gone before, so it wasn't long before Dad signaled us all to the surface.

Back on board, we marked the spot on the GPS and quickly got under way. When I mentioned my emotional experience, Zoe and Dad both said they had felt a warm surge of benevolence along with their excitement.

"Now that you mention it," Zoe said, "it felt like peace or goodwill or something."

How were we going to handle a find like this? Should we alert the authorities or keep it secret? The radio crackled and blurted half-statements about the weather as Zoe kept us on course through the oncoming storm.

"Maybe there's something to all those Triangle stories, after all," Zoe said, putting words to what we all were thinking.

One question after another came pouring out, as the three of us discussed what we should do next. We were about to reveal some real proof about something. We didn't know what, but whatever it was would be something the world had never seen. Zoe had the photo printer plugged in, so we soon had postcard-sized pictures, proof positive of our find. Dad's were darker than the two I took, but they all showed beyond a doubt that we weren't suffering from delusions. Dad checked our heading and gave the compass a couple of whacks.

"Now what?" he said. "This compass won't settle down." He looked out at the sea as the storm continued to build.

The tempestuous weather conditions reprioritized our thoughts. There was no doubt about it—a tropical storm would soon be upon us.

"We should make it back by mid-morning if we run all night," Dad said.

That was his way of asking who was taking first watch. I looked at Zoe as he pointed at me, as if to say, "*Your* turn." He was always accurate about whose watch it was.

"Right," I said, "I'll take first watch. I couldn't sleep any-way."

As we sailed on, the radio was reporting a low-pressure sys-tem heading our way a hundred miles out, but the waves were already eight feet high. When the last light left the sky, our com-pass was failing miserably, while the waves continued to build. To make matters worse, the first of a series of rogue waves came careening contrary to the general swell, threatening to capsize the boat. As we sailed into the night without a clue which way we were going, we put out a sea anchor and set the tiller.

"Let's get below," Dad said. "We'll face the night together." His words felt like a warm fire on a cold night.

The *Sea Major* was much more than just a sleek sailboat. Dad had inherited it from his lead guitar player and dear friend, Lee Vinson. They had volumes of memories and stories from their two quick years together in the late Sixties, playing and singing rock-and-roll in New York's Greenwich Village. A few years later, Lee had taken his first sailboat ride on a styrofoam sailfish while visiting Dad one summer on Coventry Lake. A year after that, Lee achieved his Sailing Master's certificate and purchased the craft, which he named *Sea Major* as a pun on the primary key of rock-and-roll.

"Lee was in his own league—you should have heard him rock," Dad would always say when telling about his phenomenal friend, prolific artist, and author of thirty-seven instructional books. "At least, he sailed to Maui and back before he left us."

Tonight she was rocking and rolling like never before. The *Sea Major*'s endurance would be tested many times before she once again saw the sun. As the tempest tore at her from all sides, all we could do was batten down and pray she passed this trial by ordeal.

"Tropical storm" was a gross understatement. Suddenly, we were in gale-force winds and thirty-foot waves. We strapped ourselves down in our bunks just in time, for the boat caught a massive wave broadside, and we capsized!

Upside-down and helpless, we bobbed torturously in the blackness.

"How long can *this* go on?" Zoe yelled.

"Come on, baby!" Dad urged. "You can do it!"

At last, we rolled again and were back in business.

"That-a-girl," Dad said, "just like you promised.... Lee told me the *Sea Major* rolled over three times on his way back from Hawaii."

But this was only our first roll. On the second one, we discovered how much we had been unable to secure in time. Everything from the galley and other quaint corners of the compartment came out to join our new spin on life.

"Use your pillows!" Dad shouted from under his.

This was proving to be an epic day—first a saucer and then a full-force gale. Our fantastic discovery was now the least of our worries as survival priorities stacked up like the waves trying to sink us. Inside the cabin, we were stirred and shaken but still mostly dry as our valiant craft denied the hurricane entry into our last bastion.

On we went, strapped inside, rolling over and over like the tumbler at nightmare bingo. After the fifth rollover, the boat wrenched and we could feel the sea anchor hang up on what must have been a reef. There was an initial jerk, but we couldn't tell if the anchor was still with us or not. The boat tossed and rolled relentlessly, and the night seemed like it would never end.

This was the worst sailing crisis we had ever been in. We all knew that the mighty little *Sea Major* could not stand this hammering much longer. But then the boat caught a monster wave and rode it like a boogie board, coming to a rocking rest on a pitch-black sandy beach.

We couldn't believe our luck as we slid out of the hatch like fresh caught tuna with a reprieve.

Torrents of driving rain made it hard to tell if we were making progress escaping from the pounding surf. Zoe now had his hazard light in his hand, which saved us from the battering waves as it revealed the shelter of palm trees and sand dunes that were out of reach of the sea. To our relief, as we made our way to the palms, the storm subsided. Grabbing what we could in the dark, we moved fifty yards onto the beach, where we collapsed and slept.

When things aren't right, there's a nasty cold feeling waiting for you when you awake. As I opened my eyes, a sinking realization of what was lost and what that meant swept over me. Looking toward the sea over sizable swells, I saw the white water from a massive wave's curl, which surfers call a "pipeline," extending across the entire horizon. While it reminded me of the pipelines off Buchanan Beach in Maui, I had never before seen one extending as far as the eye could see. It was surreal. Even more exotic were the lightning and the pea-green mist rising above the pipeline, maybe seventy or a hundred feet, before dissipating against a cloudless blue backdrop.

Looking around, I saw I was the first to wake into our new reality. What island could this be? It was somehow different. I couldn't explain it, I just had a feeling. We must have been off course the whole time.

A thunderous wave pounded ashore, startling the last bit of sleep out of me.

The boat!

I jumped up and looked toward the water. There she was.

Man, that ain't no boat no more!

I ran down to see what could be saved. The surf was up. Every wave was a water giant, pounding the beach and the boat with a constant fury. Broken but still attached by the rigging, the mast had become a battering ram. The aft section of the boat was nowhere to be seen. Our trusty *Sea Major* had saved us. In her last act of loyalty, she had taken us to shore before succumbing to the night's rage.

Luckily, we had managed to save some essentials before the pounding breakers claimed them. We had also kept our pictures of the saucer in a Ziploc baggie, and they were still dry.

Dad and Zoe were up and running toward me.

"Get everything worth saving and haul it back to where we slept!" Dad yelled.

Maybe it was because our desperate situation hadn't sunk in yet that the day's events seemed to unfold like a dream from one thing to the next. We got to work, salvaging what was left, which wasn't much. Food was not an immediate problem. We had a full case of MRE meals, as well as two flashlights, a small tarp, a sawed-off double-barreled 12-gauge shotgun, two cases of double aught buckshot, a first-aid survival kit with three flares, some rope, a fishing pole, a buck knife, a fire axe, a shortwave radio with a battery, a plastic bucket, and a half-full quart-size plastic water bottle. That was it, our entire list of assets. And only two cups of water for the three of us.

As we hauled our supplies up to where we had slept, we saw it for the first time: rising out of the jungle, shaped like a giant traffic cone, was a massive volcano.

"There's no smoke coming from it," Zoe said. "It's probably dormant."

"There might be water there," Dad speculated, "but it'll take a while to get to it. We'll look around here first. Right now let's throw a lean-to together for tonight."

After we were done building the lean-to, we spent the rest of the day searching the immediate area for water, but to no avail.

The day before, we had discovered an out-of-this-world wonder. Now we were shipwrecked. After finding a flying saucer, it seemed strange that that wasn't our main concern. Soon it would be twenty-four hours since our lives had exploded with amazement and then calamity, our world-startling discovery stifled.

Surprisingly, our mood was upbeat. I expected to be depressed. Instead, it was with very high energy that we adapted to what must be done.

We tried to radio for help, but every channel had nothing but static. Several times during the day, we tried again, but it was always the same.

There was something unreal about this place, this beach, and the combination of sun, surf, and a dormant volcano rising up through the jungle canopy, all surrounded by a thirty-foot-high pipeline. Even though this was the Atlantic Ocean, we all agreed this place seemed like some unknown South Sea island. It was the eerie green fog that hung over the pipeline and the silent silver-slivered streaks of lightning that made this place seem like a dream. It all just hung there like a permanent backdrop, suspended in midair.

We couldn't begin to explain the murky green curtain, but Dad gave it a shot: "It must be related to that pipeline somehow, like a fog or something."

"Oh, like something we've never seen before!" Zoe said. He could always be counted on to provide a little sarcastic humor, a sure sign that some things were still the same.

Dad's theory about the fog and Zoe's response closed the

subject. It was time to eat. By now, the two cups of water were long gone, so we were terribly thirsty, but no one mentioned it. Our first priority in the morning had to be water. I must admit, I was wondering how long we could go on without it before serious complications set in.

The pounding surf was hypnotic. I thought it might be too loud for sleeping.

Dad finished wiping the bucket clean with his shirt for the water we hoped to find tomorrow.

"That jungle out there," he said, "is getting its water from somewhere, so it can't be too far off. We'll find it." He knelt and made a few broad sweeps with his arm and hand in the sand. "Time to make our beds, lads, tomorrow's another day. We'll find water, I'm sure of it."

Zoe and I smiled. No matter what was happening, Dad was always an Eagle Scout. He had seen his share of tight situations as a Navy frogman, and had received two purple hearts and a silver star by the end of his tour in 1967. But he seldom spoke about those days. It was the subsequent days of flower power, 1968 and '69 that he revered, his days as a rock-and-roll singer and consummate hippie. Once, when the three of us were camping in the Sierras, he told us that even when you have to, killing is wrong, and we should never get into a situation that required it.

After the sunset illuminated the mysterious green fog over the pipeline into fascinating emerald hues, we were blanketed in the sable mantle of a moonless night sky, replete with shooting stars. We were amazed at seeing so many. As we lay back, stargazing, the view was suddenly replaced by fast approaching thunderheads rolling in.

"At least it's warm," Dad said, breaking the silence. "Things could be worse, I guess.... Goodnight, boys."

"Night, Dad," Zoe said.

And within seconds, the two of them were out like a light.

The relentless surf didn't hinder my sleep either.

I was dreaming about a steel drum band when I realized my eyes were open, and we were all sitting up. I could see us as plain as day the instant the lightning took the sky. Without a doubt, this was the most torrential downpour I had ever experienced in my life. More intense even than last night's, the rain was everywhere except on top of our heads. Our makeshift roof was keeping us dry while providing a runoff into Dad's well-placed bucket. We still hadn't fully realized the urgency of our situation. Even with the clues of the approaching storm, we were unprepared when it arrived.

"We need more water!" Dad shouted. "Rig up something to catch it in!"

Zoe was holding his MRE open to catch enough water to heat it. Dad and I scrambled around, but all we could come up with was what we already had—the bucket under the runoff from the lean-to.

As abruptly as it began, the storm subsided, and the stars reappeared. Still, our effort paid off with half a bucket of precious drinking water. We drank some and stored the rest in Dad's water bottle.

The darkest part of this, our second night was giving way to the first hints of the coming day. Sleep was over. We assumed that we must be on some vacation island because, as far as we knew, there weren't any deserted islands in this region. Besides, there was a red beam, a spotlight that seemed to be coming from behind the mountain. We thought it must be a town or resort, which we would check out at first light.

Next thing I knew, dawn was breaking and another day had begun. The spotlight was now no longer visible. We decided that following the beach would be our quickest way to find civilization. The pounding surf was a constant reminder that we were lucky to still be alive.

Dad took the tarp we were using as a roof and rearranged it to be a more effective rain catcher.

"If it pours again tonight," he said, "we'll be ready for it."

What was the story with this place? There was an eerie presence about the beach. Something felt odd. Were we really marooned, or simply down the beach from a hotel?

"This place is getting old real fast," Dad said. "We've got to find civilization today!"

His words snapped me out of my reverie.

A continuous procession of waves pounded the shore, sending tremors through the sand and up through my heels.

Zoe was trying to cast the fishing pole out beyond the shore breakers. Not having any luck, he vocalized his frustration at having gambled the beef strips in his MRE for a chance at some fresh seafood.

By now the radio was dead. It must have gotten wet, after all. Anyway, we'd probably be taking showers soon in some island resort.

"Let's not waste any more time hanging around here," Dad said. "There's probably a hotel just down the beach."

His optimism always infused us with confidence.

I sprang to my feet: "Let's get going!"

We were a motley three-man crew. Zoe carried the shotgun, I carried the boat's fire axe, and Dad had the buck knife. Not that we anticipated any violence; these were all we had for tools.

We set out down the long beach, laughing at the spectacle we would make as we wandered into the hotel, and agreeing to hide our equipment at first sight of the anticipated oasis.

All we could see was beach, surf, and jungle, but no sign of civilization. We guessed that the spotlight we had seen must have come from somewhere around the volcano.

After we had walked half an hour, the beach still seemed to keep going as far as the eye could see.

Gazing out at the water, Dad said, "That pipeline must be twenty-five to thirty feet high, from the looks of it. We must have caught the perfect wave the other night."

If it calmed down a bit, this place could be a surfers' paradise.

After a while, when we came upon an inlet, a lagoon that was cut off from the sea at the moment, we stopped dead in our tracks.

Zoe broke the spell: "Look!"

As our eyes bulged and our mouths dropped in amazement, our pace quickened.

"What's that?" I asked. "It's not real!"

We were spellbound. Despite our increased pace, we felt as though we were moving through molasses.

"Let's go!" Zoe said, charging ahead.

We were in a dead run down the beach. The closer we came, the more unbelievable the spectacle became. The lagoon was a surprise, hidden behind the sand dunes. We didn't see it until we were almost on top of it, but it was of secondary importance now to what was *in* it.

Breathless, we arrived at the lagoon's edge, standing knee deep in the sun-warmed water. We were transfixed, trying to understand that, half buried in the sand in ten feet of water, was a huge frigate!

On a thirty-degree pitch, it stood there with fragments of sails and rigging blowing in the trade winds. It was thrilling to see this authentic movie prop, if that's what it was. From where we stood, there was nothing else to indicate what her story might be.

"This must be one heck of a resort!" Zoe said.

"I don't think so," I said. "More like a movie set..., looks too real."

Shaking his head after a hard look, Dad weighed in: "That's no movie set, boys, we've found something here! That thing is *real*! Judging from the droop of that weathered wood and the tatters hanging off her riggings, it looks to me like she's been here a long time…, maybe a hundred years or more. It doesn't seem possible, but there it is!"

Zoe was chafing at the bit. "Yeah, there it is alright, but what are we gonna *do* about it?"

The waves were hammering the shore behind us, an impatient reminder that we needed to address our priorities. But that reminder went unheeded.

"Let's just swim right out there," Zoe said.

"That wouldn't be *my* first choice," Dad replied. "There might be something in the water."

We decided to fashion a raft to float the fifty yards or so out to the ancient wreck. This diversion consumed most of the day. Searching about, we found a couple of sizable tree trunks just beyond the tree line, which we barely managed to roll to the edge of the lagoon. Retrieving the rope from camp, we lashed the two ancient boles together and were delighted to find them able to support us and remain buoyant.

By the time we found some poles, the sun had begun its downward slant, so we decided to hold off until tomorrow. Leaving our untried water taxi and poles ready for the next day's trip, we hiked back to the lean-to for food and rest.

Sleep didn't come as easily as it had the night before. There was too much to think about.

How long will it be before we get back to civilization? How long has that frigate been here? A hundred years or more, Dad said.

A flush of desperation overtook me as I realized that this

island might be unknown!

How can that be? And what's with that strange pipeline that never ends?

One thing was certain—we were on some kind of odyssey. Tomorrow we were going to board a nineteenth-century frigate and try to unravel her story…and ours.

"Sun's up!" Zoe shouted.

I could tell in those two spoken words that he was psyched for what was to come.

Dad was adding sea water to heat his MRE. "We need to locate a water supply as soon as possible," he said. "It should be pretty easy to find in the jungle."

"Yeah," Zoe said, "but that can wait just a little longer. First, let's board that frigate and check it out. There might even be some water aboard."

"Okay," Dad said, "we'll make a quick recon first, but it's unlikely we'll find any fresh water on that boat."

By now we were walking fast, but at the first glimpse of the lagoon and its secret, we started running toward our tree trunk gondola. Our urgent situation didn't seem to weigh in as the excitement and anticipation pushed thoughts of water aside for the moment. We straddled our tree trunk raft, one behind the other. It would be a short sail through the warm waters out to whatever was waiting for us.

With poles in position, Dad gave the word, "Shove off!"

Maneuvering wasn't as hard as I thought it would be. The poles worked well, since the bottom was only eight or nine feet deep. When we were thirty yards out, the details on the frigate became clearer: *Tortuga Diablo* was her name.

This was the real McCoy—simple, solid construction with two thirty-foot masts and a foremast. There were two decks of cannon doors, most of which were closed, but a few were open, exposing the cannons. With ten guns on each deck, she had to have at least forty cannons.

We came along the low side, which presented the best opportunity to board. From this vantage point, the weather deck and the helm were in plain view. The great masts were still intact. I was surprised to see the design was plain, lacking any scrolling or other embellishments on its woodwork. The entire forward skeleton of the ship, except for the two gun decks, was exposed and flooded. All the ship's lumber on the starboard side had been removed, but it wasn't evident where the wood had gone.

"What do you think happened to the wood?" I asked.

"The sailors might have used it to construct shelters," Dad said, "or maybe build a raft or something to get off the island."

The exposed bracing had the same dusky hue as the rest of the ship, indicating that the cannibalization had happened some time ago. As we climbed aboard the frigate from the raft, we were eager to see what we would find.

"If we're lucky, there may be some treasure aboard," Zoe said.

"If we were lucky," I said, "we wouldn't be here at all."

Walking on the ship's deck was hard on our ankles, for a thirty-degree pitch is a mean slant. As we made our way toward the helm, we strained to walk upright. Even so, it was intoxicating to be standing on this ancient deck in its final resting place. There was something eerie about this decaying ship, which gave us an inexplicable sense of foreboding.

"I wonder where she came from," I said.

"Yeah?" Zoe said. "How about *when* she came from?"

His quick response startled the butterflies in my stomach as we continued toward the bridge.

"There are no flags or insignias," Dad said. "I think she was a private ship..., possibly a pirate ship!"

We found the helm to be intact. As Zoe turned the big wheel, Dad walked to the stern and leaned over the taffrail.

"I can see the chains tugging at the frozen rudder," he shouted.

The doors to what must have been the captain's quarters opened with little effort, rustling the musty air and doubling the light that was allowed by the aft bank of windows. Patina covered every surface of the macabre chamber. It appeared that there had been little, if any, disturbance to the moldering trappings of the tomblike quarters of the ship's master. Like some morbid pantomime, the whole scene was silently screaming a story of foul play. There in the center of the grand cabin was a long table with only one dinner guest.

"Could this be the captain?" Zoe wondered aloud about the

remains sprawled out over the table, but still sitting in the chair.

Dad pointed to another skeleton in the captain's bed. It was obvious from the clothing that the skeleton perched on the disintegrating bedclothes was a woman, just as the one at the table was a man. The woman on the bed had a flintlock pistol next to her. We could only imagine what had been going on the night these folks sailed into the lagoon.

Our romantic hope of finding some treasure was dispelled by the grim reality that now confronted us. The gruesome scene in the captain's quarters was dispiriting, giving the *Tortuga Diablo* an eerie hue of treachery that tainted our idyllic first impression.

Dad was growing impatient. "More puzzle parts, too many for now," he said. "We've got other problems. First of all, we've gotta find water. Let's finish up this recon and take care of business."

We got busy taking a quick inventory. There were thirty-eight cannons on the two gun decks, twenty barrels of shot, and too many barrels of black powder to count. The armory had a dozen barrels of flints, a few flintlocks in the rack, but no pistols anywhere. Whatever treasure or valuables there had been on board were gone. That the ship was flooded below the second gun deck suggested that there might be something of value lying on the bottom in the sand, but we weren't going to think about that now. With the day half over, we were far from our MREs and wearing thin.

As we looked back from the edge of the lagoon, the *Tortuga*

Diablo was still a breathtaking sight. Although we now knew some of her secrets, the possibilities of her story spread in my imagination like wildfire.

We decided to go a little farther down the beach and then penetrate the jungle, returning by the tree line. The cloudless sky and the blazing sun lit the briny aquamarine swells that pummeled the golden beaches, reminding me of our Tahitian brother Miko's description of his home.

As we walked along and talked about everything, I almost forgot that we were on a survival mission. Despite our thirst, our excitement perpetuated an illusion that this odyssey would sustain us, no matter what. It was bizarre to be in such dire straits while still enjoying the adventure. The idea that we would stumble onto a resort scene now seemed remote at best.

At the edge of the jungle, we turned back toward the camp. The teeming rain forest was ringing with its denizens' clamor. Zoe went a hundred yards into the trees, I went in fifty yards, and Dad walked along the tree line. Using our paintball calls, we signaled back and forth to each other, but otherwise remained quiet as we went in search of any clue that could lead us to water.

We had been silent for a while when Zoe's arctic owl call pierced the hypnotic drone beneath the canopy. He was signaling us in. Moving toward him, we heard a tom-tom or conga, some kind of drumbeat under a plaintive sound like a chant, a wail, and a cry all in one — not threatening, but rather haunting. The wail rose above the denizens' clatter. Inching along, we were a good two hundred yards in from the beach as we hacked our way through the tiresome undergrowth.

Zoe saw him first. "Jackpot!" he said in a hushed tone. "It's a hippie singing by a brook!"

The profusion of jungle flora made it impossible for me to see what Zoe was looking at. I thought maybe the resort thing was happening, after all. By the time Dad joined us, Zoe and I were standing ten yards behind the hippie, who, all this time, never missed a beat and seemed unaware of us, even as we approached him.

"Italian?" I said.

We looked at each other, delighted and amazed, for he was singing in our second language! Dad had taught us Italian when we were kids. By the time Zoe, Shanda, and I were teenagers, our wide exposure to Italian culture and conversation had us fluent in our grandparents' native tongue. Shanda, now a mother of two, insists it was her ability to speak the language and teach Italian cooking that brought her and her husband together. Funny I should be thinking of my kid sister at this moment. We'd been going back to visit her and Craig on Martha's Vineyard every September for the last three years. They seemed so far away now as I wondered when we would ever see them again. The beckoning chant was compelling, bringing me back into the present.

With the brook before us, our crisis was over. Now we had all the water we could ever use. The rippling crystal-clear stream's promise soothed our thirst even before we tasted it. The one who had guided us to it had us equally captivated.

When he finally saw us, he wasn't startled. Although he

smiled, he never stopped his chant or his beat.

As if Dad had been there forever, he smiled back and, after quenching his thirst, sat down and listened. We followed Dad's lead.

Zoe's first impression of the singer had been reasonable. Maybe he *was* a hippie. His forehead was painted yellow and orange. His cheeks wore green and blue streaks. A thin headband held back his flowing black hair. A turquoise necklace, a toga of ochre, and sandals that laced up the calves had all been trappings attributed to flower power.

Intent on his task, he continued singing (in Italian):

> *We have one thing in common*
> *With all there can be*
> *Everything everywhere*
> *From the stars to the flea*
> *We are the raindrops*
> *We are the sea*
> *We are all the One called Me.*

The hippie put his drum down, looking at us and past us at the same time.

"*Pace a voi*," he said.

His acknowledgment, which meant "Peace to you," sounded like something a hippie would say.

"*Pace a te!*" we answered.

The clamor of jungle residents was jarring. This far into the forest, the canopy was layers thick, providing dark cooling shade to the delicious, pure waters of the life-saving stream. Now that our water problems were over, the presence of this Italian balladeer seemed to suggest that help was not far away.

With a curious half-smile, he asked in Italian, "Have you come to help me?"

Our realities clashed. Where was this guy coming from, asking *us* for help? He had just saved our lives, bringing us to the water here, much further in than we would have ventured had we not heard his beckoning chant. His question had the hope of a lost child—not what we wanted to hear. Still, he made us want to help him if we could. He was starting to realize we weren't the people he thought we were. His expression took on a grim uneasiness.

Sensing his angst, Zoe asked, "What's your name, brother?"

Looking into Zoe's eyes, he answered, "Themi."

"Maybe we *can* help you," Zoe said, "but we're lost, too. Where are we? What island is this?"

As the revitalizing waters rippled by, soothing the anxious moment, we waited for an answer. But Zoe's questions went unacknowledged, for Themi's eyes were searching our faces as he tried to place us.

With a faint smile, he finally answered, "Where *are* we? We are *here*. We are here, sitting on the Wizard's Hat. I came here to cry. They forgot about me. When they remember, they'll come and get me. I guess I was sleeping. I've lost my direction. I can't find my way back in."

He reached into his sack and produced a cone-shaped bowl, covered with markings. Turning it over, he studied it like a map. Dad, Zoe, and I exchanged glances.

"What is this guy saying?" Zoe asked.

"He lost me right after *Pace a voi*," I replied.

"He's talking to us one minute," Zoe said, "and looking past us the next."

"Look's like he's *on* something," Dad said, making a quick hand-to-eye gesture, meaning he looked a little too wide-eyed.

I urged Zoe on: "Try him again."

Themi was still preoccupied with the bowl, turning it as if he were looking for some mark that was missing.

"When did you get here, brother?" Zoe asked.

But no answer came. Instead, from the distant blackness beneath the canopy, a bloodcurdling shriek silenced the jungle clamor. We all stood up, petrified. The gargantuan roar instantly dissolved any luster this place had, leaving only terror lurking in every shadow. It was evident that the jungle was populated by a wide variety of carnivores, and that was bad enough. This latest addition to the chorus added a whole new dimension of possibilities.

Themi leaned over and picked up his drum. Although he tried to appear indifferent, it was clear he was not. Turning away from where the hideous cry originated, he said, "I'll sing *Buona Sera, Lamoria….* Surely they'll hear that."

A new, louder, more intense rhythm introduced his next selection as he projected its urgent message:

Buona sera, Lamoria
The cosmic night approaches
It's as long as the day
We will sleep unstirring
Lest we steal away.

He repeated the hypnotic chant over and over as he beat his drum.

"Where does this guy fit in?" Dad said.

"He's waiting for friends," I said. "Somebody to come and take him back home."

Zoe was becoming annoyed: "What's he trying to do, attract that monster out there?"

The hippie finished his chant, turned to us, and said, "They must have heard me that time. It shouldn't be long now."

"This guy's in deep denial," Zoe said. "How could this chant serve any purpose?" He tried another question on the bewildered balladeer: "How far away are your people?"

This time, after a pause, the hippie answered, "We can never get back to Mu."

Zoe shot back, "What *is* this place?"

"This place is Crystal Mountain..., the Wizard's Hat."

"When did you come here?"

"I'm lost. They must have gone in and forgotten about me. I can't find the way back in."

Zoe threw up his hands. "Here we go again." Turning back to us, he said, "One thing is certain, this dude is lost. I can't understand anything he says."

Dad had that quitting time look in his eyes. "Right," he said. "Well, I don't think we can help this guy. It's getting late…, only a couple hours of light left…, so, what are we gonna do?"

Dad usually *told* us what to do, but every once in a while, he would switch, and it would be our call.

"Food's a long walk from here," I said. "Let's go back to the lean-to, eat, and relocate to here in the morning."

Zoe nodded, then looked back at Themi, who was kneeling at the brook: "What about *this* guy?"

Themi was taking a drink from the brook with the same bowl he had been studying a moment before. Looking in one direction and then another, he stuffed his bowl away in his side sack.

Beneath the copious jungle canopy, it was becoming darker by the minute, and I, for one, didn't want to be here after sunset.

All at once, the hippie stood up as if his ride were arriving. "I wish they would come now," he said. "I want to go back." With that, he sat down, clutching his drum.

Now Dad tried his luck: "We're hungry, brother. Do you have anything to eat?"

"I am on a fast," he said. "Water and dreamers only."

As he answered, he reached into the satchel he had slung to one side and produced what looked to us like grapes.

Rolling his eyes, Zoe said, "No wonder he's dazed! A few of those probably make things look different for a while."

Zoe's attempt at humor seemed to concern Themi.

"Who *are* you?" he asked. "I don't know *you!*"

Once again, he scrutinized us as we tried to explain.

"We are sailors," Dad said, "and we were shipwrecked not far from here. We're from California."

Themi's lips became tight and thin as he shot back, "Your words mean nothing. Why do you talk that way? I know it is forbidden to be outside on the mountain."

Themi's concern was not driven by fear. Rather, he was impatient with our incomprehensible response.

Dad continued, "*What* don't you understand?"

Themi was very focused now. "Shipwrecked sailors," he said, "I've never heard of the place you say you are from. Why talk to me like this?"

His eyes were glaring like flaming swords. The tone he had taken was echoed by the forest denizens.

Dad extended his hands, a gesture to calm Themi down. "Even though we are having trouble understanding each other," he said, "we mean you no harm. We are confused by things you say. Are we not near the sea?"

Themi looked at us as if we were crazy. "You should know how far we are from the sea," he said, "if you truly came from there."

Dad continued in a gentle tone: "It will be dark soon. We just have time to make it back to our camp. You are welcome to come with us tonight. We plan to relocate back here tomorrow."

Themi wasn't about to go camping with us. You could see it in his eyes as he turned away, picked up his drum, and put another twenty feet between himself and us before choosing another bole. He sat huddled, shaking his head.

"Goodbye," Dad said. "*Buona sera.* We'll be back here in the morning."

As we started back the way we had come, Themi gave a single wave before the jungle swallowed him up.

"That dude is on a vision quest or something," said Zoe. "What did he say that we can make sense of?"

I knew Zoe's question was rhetorical, but I answered anyway: "Not much. Maybe if we had some of those dreamers he was eating, we would all have been on the same page."

Zoe shook his head. "I doubt that would have done the trick."

"Do you think he'll be there tomorrow?" I asked.

Dad made a whisking hand motion. "We'll see tomorrow. Right now, let's put a move on…, it's getting dark."

The sable mantle of night began to settle under the canopy as a blazing red dome confirmed the setting sun. The daunting sounds in the shadows sent a jagged current of cold apprehension up our spines, providing extra glide to our stride as the pounding surf, like a distant drum, grew louder. When we broke out of the jungle onto the beach, we marked the spot with a pile of palm leaves and brush.

Pointing back toward the mountain stream, Dad said, "*That's where the water is!*"

Now that we were out of the canopy, we still had an hour of daylight left. The thunderous pummeling of the surf felt like a familiar haven as it replaced the hideous din of the steaming jungle.

By now, we were walking fast down the beach. When we came to the lagoon, the frigate was a dark amber silhouette. We passed it by like the corner drugstore on our way home. Mission accomplished for today. Tomorrow had a whole new list of things to do before we could leave this place.

"What a week!" Dad said. "First, a flying saucer, then a pirate ship.... All this and shipwrecked too!" His words billowed as we chugged along.

"Look there!" Zoe said, stopping. He was pointing to a precipice on the hills behind the lagoon. "There it is again..., a flicker, a fire..., definitely a fire. A campfire? This place is getting crowded. Maybe it's the hippie's friends."

His attempt to solve this latest mystery didn't quell my fear of the unknown.

"We'll check that out tomorrow," Zoe said, resuming his pace. "Maybe Themi knows about the campfire."

"Maybe," I said, "if we can understand what he says about it."

I wondered how Themi was doing right now. His decision to remain alone in the ominous nocturnal jungle demonstrated our failure to communicate.

Just then, a familiar sight came into view.

"There's home, boys!" Dad shouted. "Let's eat!" His words felt like a pair of snug socks on a cold winter's night.

A lone lean-to on a desolate beach, the little camp actually felt like home as we anticipated the comforts waiting for us.

The MREs tasted great. Perhaps it was our situation that made them taste so good, but whatever it was, they never tasted better.

After dinner we sat around, trying to figure out what was happening on this island with frigates, lagoons, lost hippies, and scary jungles. Fatigue and the night sky finally rendered us speechless. Comets and shooting stars illuminated the heavens in a captivating celestial rapture unlike anything we had ever seen. Gazing up, we drifted into an enchanted sleep.

Boom! Boom!

The ground beneath my sleeping head suddenly slapped me awake. It was not an explosion, but an earthquake!

Boom! Boom!

Each loud thud came with its own tremor.

The three of us jumped to our feet.

"JEE-zus!"

Dad's favorite exclamation of surprise pierced the night, focusing us on the problem.

As we looked seaward under the moonless starry sky, we could see something—a creature bigger than an elephant. Its hulking silhouette was passing by our camp. As it walked, we bounced with each step.

"Some kind of dinosaur," Dad whispered. "Maybe a T.rex."

It was definitely a biped, a good twenty-five or thirty feet tall—a carnivore, as we could see from its silhouetted rows of incisors. The beast let loose a familiar ghastly roar, momentarily drowning out the thundering surf.

There was no doubt that this was the author of the horrific bellow we had heard in the jungle on the previous afternoon. Right out of a horror scene, this wasn't a dream. It just didn't seem possible to be this close to something that was supposed to have been extinct millions of years ago.

When fear and vulnerability come together, they freeze the spine with terror. As the monster walked by us, we were as still as the sand. The wind was in our favor, so we went unnoticed as it passed between the pounding surf and us, leaving us like three survivors in hell.

"Now dinosaurs!" Zoe whispered. "Man, this place is jumping!"

As we watched the black hulk move down the beach out of sight, Dad's tone was grim: "I wonder how many of *them* are on this island."

His words were sobering, if not ominous. I longed to hear that carefree tone he had the other night, about a week and a world ago. He had been laughing and telling us that we were true sailors of fortune, free to roam the seven seas in search of the eighth wonder of the world. Now it seemed that his prophecy of finding that wonder was manifesting right before our eyes.

As sailors of fortune, we had somehow crossed over into a new dimension of outrageous circumstances, which included flying saucers, pirate ships, and dinosaurs. If this were a dream, why couldn't I wake up? And yet, what else could it be? All these fantastic occurrences, one after another, made me wonder if we weren't already dead.

"Man, what are we gonna do if we come up against one of *those* things?" Zoe said.

Sleep was impossible now. We all sat deep in our own thoughts, waiting for the morning light.

As the sun appeared on the horizon, I wondered what would happen next. We collected our gear, taking only what was essential: weapons, ammo, MREs, flashlights, and our pictures of the flying saucer.

Following our plan, we started out for the brook. After last night's visitor, we realized that the beach camp was far too vulnerable. We would have to take our chances in the ominous jungle. At least there was water there.

On the beach, halfway to our marker, we came across footprints as big as a VW bug and three feet deep. We could see the path it had made where it came out of the tree line. We quickened our pace as we passed "Big Bertha's" enormous tracks.

Things felt different now. A real dinosaur was not romantic. Knowing such a creature was here infused us with a jagged feeling of helplessness.

"What *else* is on this island?" Zoe said.

We were so intent on those giant tracks in the sand that we went right by the lagoon and frigate without noticing. As I mentioned this to Dad, Zoe reminded us of the campfire we had seen last night.

"We'll check it out, but first things first," Dad said, spurring us on. "Let's get to the brook and plan our next move."

When we came upon our marker, it was exactly as we had left it, and our tracks from the day before were still fresh. As we penetrated the jungle, we could see things had changed in the night. A cleared path of destruction ten or twelve feet wide was left by the monster. Complete with the signature footprints, the path of rubble led back toward the brook. Intermittent shafts of amber light penetrated the dense canopy to the plush forest floor, enhancing the savage beauty of this Stygian habitat.

The clangorous feral chorus indicated that it was just another day in this steaming hellhole. I heard the brook before I saw it because the rubble had almost covered it over. We could barely tell that this was the same spot we had been at yesterday. Broken trees were strewn about where "Bertha" had put her big feet. Now there was a small pond in the middle of the stream.

"If Themi isn't hanging around anymore," Zoe said, "I can understand why."

We looked about, trying to see where Themi might be. The trampled path made travel easier in most spots. Even so, this jungle highway wasn't worth the chance that we might have to pay the pathmaker.

Dad was about twenty yards upstream when we heard him yell, "JEE-zus!"

It wasn't swearing. He had told us many times that it was more of a prayer.

As we scrambled toward him, we could see that he was looking up at something caught in the trees.

"Let's go, boys, we're outta here!" he said, giving us that if-you-know-what's-good-for-you look.

He spun and started back downstream, but it was too late. We had already seen what was left of Themi. There wasn't much—a partial torso, barely recognizable, caught in a treetop like a snagged kite.

I looked away, but not fast enough. Images of Themi's gruesome fate forced themselves into my mind along with the script for my next nightmare.

A moment later, Zoe found Themi's sack with the ornate drinking bowl.

"Take it along," Dad said. "And let's get the hell outta here!"

His orders gave me a queasy feeling as I tried to come to grips with what was happening. Things were moving at a furious pace, and there was no time for reflection.

Zoe was somber as he considered Dad's orders. "Outta here?" he asked. "Where to?"

"Let's follow the brook back toward the lagoon," Dad said. "At least, we'll have water...and besides, that was our next point of interest. We'll try to find out what that fire was all about last night."

He was struggling to sound positive.

Zoe needed more. His eyes were glassy, and his face looked vacant and older.

"Where in hell are we?" he said. "This is no normal place…. It's full of questions without answers."

Putting his arm around Zoe's shoulders, Dad looked into his eyes and spoke in the golden tones of a loving father: "There's gotta be some answers to all of this, son. We'll figure this out…, so let's get moving and see what we can find."

"Yeah," Zoe rebounded, "before it finds *us*."

He couldn't resist getting the last word in, but Dad let it slide.

Zoe slung the poor dead hippie's sack over his shoulder, and we were off.

"Our luck is due for a change," Dad said. "It's time to find out who or what is behind that campfire we saw. Maybe we'll find some friendlies there."

His words were like firecrackers on deaf ears. It was only his love that gave us flight.

"Stay sharp, boys!"

We were moving through the jungle in stealth mode. Silence would be our ally as the steaming virgin forest reverberated with the desperate sounds of fear and hunger. The stream seemed to be going toward the lagoon. Even though it twisted at times, it always turned back that way. Although the thick jungle canopy darkened our path with deep shadows, we could see a clearing just ahead. The stream continued through the opening and back into the jungle. When we reached the clearing, we stopped.

I noticed that the hairs on the back of my neck were standing on end. When I mentioned this to Dad, he said, "Yeah, I feel it, too."

Zoe instinctively took the point, with the 12-gauge at the ready.

The clearing seemed more like a park than a jungle. The tiny open meadow was pastoral with green grass, wildflowers, and—

"Blackberries!" Zoe yelled.

There in the center of the clearing was an enormous stand of enticing splendor. Maybe Dad's prediction was coming true. Mostly ripe and glistening in the sun, the berries were the size of walnuts. They were the best we ever tasted, sweet and juicy. We ate them until we couldn't eat anymore. For a moment, we almost forgot where we were.

Zoe went over to check out the far side of the clearing when, all of a sudden, my face was being scratched by blackberry thorns as I was slammed to the ground face-first!

Awwk! Awwwk!

I rolled over in time to see a huge black bird. Its fifteen-foot wingspan generated a micro-cyclone, engulfing me in dust and debris as its deadly talons grasped for my flesh. I didn't know it at the time, but Dad was also down and under attack.

Zoe was a hundred feet away when he heard the commotion and saw what was happening. In a flash, he came running with the shotgun.

Kaboom! Kaboom!

He must have fired for effect, because I knew he wasn't in range yet, and he knew it, too.

Forest Fox: *Pirates of Marauda*

As the big bird came at me again, I kicked with both feet at its belly. When the beast flinched for a moment, I rolled toward my fire ax. Zoe ran right past me as I got to my feet. This time I met my foe with a full swing, and the ax dug in. As I hung on with both hands, the blade came away from its mark.

Dad had much the same experience. He kept his aggressor off until Zoe ran right up to within two feet of the bird and gave it both barrels.

Kaboom! Kaboom!

Zoe reloaded his gun in a cloud of smoke and huge black feathers. As Dad's assailant collapsed, I looked for mine, but it was gone. As abruptly as the attack had begun, it was over.

Dad was none the worse for the scuffle — at least, physically. We were both scratched and bleeding, more from the thorns than the humongous birds.

"JEE-zus!" Dad exclaimed. "This place has got some nasty surprises! I never heard them coming." He was on his feet now and looking all around. "Let's stay sharp, boys! We're no more than mice to those birds."

We gathered some more blackberries before moving on. Until a few minutes ago, we weren't even thinking about birds, but now we noticed that there was a distinct absence of smaller creatures in the area.

After collecting and checking our gear, we continued downstream and back into the sanctuary of the canopy. We still had plenty of MREs left, so we never considered cleaning and cooking Zoe's kill. The grotesque events of the morning and the un-

70

nerving battle with the birds over their blackberries made the path to our next objective seem longer than we anticipated.

Dad tried his best to keep up our morale. "If we can find that dinner fire tonight," he said, "we might get invited."

His optimism was like a squirt gun in a grass fire, but for the moment, it would have to do.

As we walked along, I noticed that Zoe hadn't said a word since the blackberries. Even though he always performs under pressure with the precision of a commando, this jaunt through the jungle was clearly depressing him. In another mile, however, he broke his silence.

"I haven't seen any animals smaller than us," he said, looking around as he spoke. "And this crazy brook! It zigzags, but it doesn't seem to be going downhill at all."

To keep up Zoe's spirits, Dad sang a couple of bars:

> *Ol' Man River, that Ol' Man River,*
> *It just keeps rollin' along....*

"This brook is a great water source," he said. "That makes it the best friend we've got here so far."

Dad had made his point. This water was pure and refreshing. As we followed our new best friend, we tried to make sense of this surrealistic chain of events. The only thing we could come up with was the Bermuda Triangle theory, or that we were all having the same nightmare. Either way, we were caught like characters in the *Twilight Zone*.

Under the canopy, the ever-present racket was intimidating as we continued along the lush, shaded path that led to a lookout point. From there we could see that we were now a hundred feet above the beach below. The frigate in the lagoon was partially visible in the distance.

The savage landscape of this place was mesmerizing. However, knowing the potential for terror that lurked in every shadow stifled any enjoyment of the view.

Dad pointed up toward an outcropping of trees a hundred feet above us on a precipice that was overgrown with hanging vegetation.

"The fire we saw last night," he said, "must have been up in that area. Look for a path."

We started up with Zoe on point. The climb was steep, but we could see that there was no shortage of good footholds. Although ascending with gear wasn't easy, we made steady progress. Clinging to the steep sides of the precipice, we managed to scale fifty feet closer to our objective.

Suddenly, the jungle din was pierced by a single report that rang out somewhere above us. We must have looked as if the ground had gone out from under us as we dropped for cover—an instinct we had developed from years of playing paintball.

"Up there about two o'clock," I whispered, pointing to a small cloud of white smoke floating on the breeze about thirty-five feet above us.

"I don't think he was shooting at us!" Dad responded.

He was probably right. It was a single shot with no verbal

warning.

"Maybe a hunter," I suggested.

"That's as good a guess as any," Dad said. His eyes had that hunter's look, intent and squinted, meaning that we were on our way to some action, and there would be a prize.

The jungle clatter was starting to resume when a second shot exploded like a thunderclap.

This time we only flinched as another white puff dissipated in the breeze.

"That was about the same place as last time," Dad said, watching the smoke as it disappeared. "He's not shooting at us."

Zoe quickly checked his gun and snapped it shut, then slung it over his shoulder.

"Let's go!" Dad said.

Because the next section of the climb wasn't as arduous, we were able to move faster. After five minutes, there were no more shots, so we lost our fix on the shooter.

Then our hunt was over when a clearing took us by surprise. Zoe was the first to reach it. His hand went up, signaling us to stop. We stayed unmoving, wondering what he saw.

"A fort," Zoe whispered loudly.

When we crept closer, it came into view. The stockade had a perimeter wall of fifteen-foot poles—trees cut to fit for a snug barrier. We could only see the one wall before us, which extended two hundred feet to the edge of a sheer cliff above the beach. From our position, we weren't able to see the whole layout.

"At last, *people!*" Zoe said. "Now we'll get some answers!"

"Okay, boys, easy does it," Dad said, reining us in. "Be quiet until we know what's happening. Let's find the front door and figure out whether or not we wanna come calling."

Dad was right. These guys might be some kind of desperados. We would stay unannounced until we could be sure. Following Dad's hand signal, we moved out. Working our way down along the wall of rough-cut tree trunks, we came to the first corner of what we assumed was a rectangular blockade. There were no windows or gunports of any kind.

Then we heard a male voice on the other side of the fortress walls: "Heave! Heave! Heave! That's good enough…. Tie it off!"

Whatever they were doing, it was clear they were not aware of us. We listened for more talk, something to give us a hint of the type of people we could expect to find within. Continuing on around the first corner, we found a closed gate. The entry was as tall as the wall itself and only distinguishable by its cross members. We crouched into the vegetation fifteen feet away to become invisible.

"We'll wait and watch who comes and goes," Dad said.

His plan, however, was interrupted by what could only have been a deliberate loud snap—a branch or twig close behind us.

Once again, the hairs on the back of my neck came to attention.

"Avast!" said a raspy voice. "Don't do anythin' foolish now, or I'll be sendin' ya on to glory!"

The voice felt like crushed ice as it shocked me into comprehension. Obviously, our attempt at concealment had been ineffective. Whoever it was, was right behind us.

I had a terrible sinking feeling, being surprised like this, but it was mixed with curiosity about what the owner of this voice might look like. His phrasing was right out of a pirate movie.

As the speaker came around to face us, we all raised our hands. He looked the part alright, earring and all. About thirty years old, he stood before us, pointing a flintlock and staring with a fiery gaze. It was another moment in our unraveling odyssey that seemed more like a dream than reality.

"What do we 'ave 'ere?" he said. "Three explorers come to claim the island of the damned for yourselves, says I!"

There was an awkward silence as we tried to come to grips with what was happening. From the ancient flintlock and his red berry skin to the cutlass and scabbard on the side of his striped cutaways, this guy was dressed for a part he was not playing.

Smiling, Zoe fell right into his role in this bizarre situation. First, under his breath, he said to us, "Look at that piece." Then, stepping out as if he might make a move, he said aloud, "Aye, mate, shipwrecked and lost we be. This island is unknown to us. We were hoping to find some mates to help us get back home."

Our captor's response to Zoe softened our first impression of his intent. Zoe's words seemed a bit comical to him. A faint smile and then a twinkle in his eye emerged as he continued his interrogation: "Sailors, says you? What ship?"

"The *Sea Major*," Zoe replied. "A forty-foot yawl we used

for treasure hunting."

"Aye, treasure. Well now, that be somethin' we 'ave in common. But treasure has no place 'ere on the island of the damned."

His words left us dumbfounded.

"Alright," he said, "it's off to see the captain with ya. Shove off!"

He pointed toward the fort, and then gestured with his rifle for us to go ahead as he hollered out to those behind the wall, "Open the gate!"

His call did not get an immediate response, but as we reached the entrance, the tall gate opened. We entered the courtyard, where we could see that the interior had a lived-in feeling despite the maze of pointed poles aimed skyward everywhere in the stockade.

There were two men to the left, who were butchering a great bird that was much like the one that had attacked us. They had it hanging from a tall rack designed just for that purpose.

Their eyes followed us as we proceeded toward the main structure, whose presence solved the mystery of the missing lumber of the *Tortuga Diablo*. Irregular in its design, the structure had an uncomplicated charm. Stairs led up to the second floor, which had a spiked railing. The name *Tortuga Diablo* appeared on a plaque next to the stairway.

As we reached the steps, we saw a man who could have been a stand-in for Errol Flynn in *Captain Blood*.

Our first impression vanished when we heard his thunderous

baritone: "What have you there, more citizens of Limbo?"

Our escort replied, "Aye, Cap'n, found 'em in the bush outside the gate, I did."

The captain stood in the shade as we were introduced. When he turned into the light, his gaunt image was exposed, revealing a tormented man of thirty-five years or so. He was wide-eyed, as if he were seeing a reality that we were not aware of, his forehead laden with the wrinkles of his perception. His eyes pierced us with their intensity and, accompanied by his voice, gave our hearts a jolt.

"Well, now, welcome to the island of the damned.... Aye, where nature practices a perverted fury!"

I didn't know if he was greeting us or condemning us. It sounded like a little of each.

Unflinching, Dad took a step forward. "We are sailors like yourselves," he said, "shipwrecked and wandering about. Can you tell us where we are, Captain?"

Staring across the courtyard through the clustered pointed poles, the captain answered us in fateful and tormented tones. "*Where* are we? *When* are we? It's well over a hundred years since that storm out there put us here. This place can't be found on any map. It's a savage place, where life is a sentence that can only be terminated by the titans that rule here!"

His speech had us riveted. His face was like a volcano as his words splashed our understanding with molten amazement.

The captain's tone turned bitter: "This be Limbo.... Orders given, orders obeyed."

He definitely had a case of what Dad called the "wide eyes."

Comprehending the looks on our faces, he bellowed, "Aye, madness is the true face of immortality. You don't understand… we're already dead. We died long ago in that storm yonder. This island is that place between heaven and hell, prison of the titans, Limbo of the damned, where the gods cast those who are to be forgotten."

Dad turned toward us. His glare said it all. This guy was serious! His declaration had us shaking in our boots with apprehension. His delivery left no doubt about his instability. His choice of words, however, seemed reasonable, and that was the worst part of it. When he finished, the silence was profound. He looked at one of the others, a stocky swarthy salt.

"Show them where to stow their gear," he said.

"Aye, Captain," came the reply, and the captain disappeared into the house.

Our guide pointed to a hooch over in one corner of the courtyard. "That way, mates."

The fury of the moment dissipated. The pirates showed no concern for our potential as adversaries. After the captain's fiery greeting, it was as though we were new crewmembers as he dispatched us to quarters. There were eight other shelters scattered about, some occupied. Ours was furthest from the captain's quarters.

"We appreciate the hospitality," said Dad.

At first, his comment drew no response from our guide as we followed him to the hooch. Then, turning, and with a half-smile, he melted the awkward silence. "I am James Villa," he said. Pointing at the hooch, he added, "You can have this one." Then, as he walked off toward the men dressing the giant turkey, he said, "We'll all have a talk later, after supper."

The stockade felt secure, with its three fifteen-foot-high walls of double thick timbers. A sheer three-hundred-foot drop to the beach below made a fourth wall unnecessary. It was from this angle that we had seen the fire from the beach the night before. There were eighteen-foot pointed poles everywhere, not more than five feet apart.

"Their function must be to prevent attacks from above," Zoe speculated.

"At least, inside this stockade, the jungle racket is muffled," I said, "and that's alright with me."

From the doorway, Dad said, "These guys seem okay. I guess they're considering us guests. No one even noticed our weapons, let alone confiscated them. Best of all, they've invited us to dinner."

Our hooch was fifteen feet by ten, with a single door, a thatched roof, and straw mats on the floor. As we looked out, the fort appeared adequate and comfortable. There were several hammocks in one area around a fire pit. The man who opened the gate was tending the coals. We counted three other men besides the captain and Villa in the compound. There was the butcher (who had brought us in), the gate man, and one other, who was making sawing and hammering noises somewhere behind our hooch.

Zoe had that faraway look again. "How can it be," he said, "that they have been here over a hundred years and still look so young?" His question was riveting, and the answer was probably going to be bad news.

Dad chose optimism over rationality. "Well," he said, "if that's their ship in the lagoon, what they're saying must be true. But whatever the case may be, I don't think we need to go into it. I suggest that we just be here now and wait for things to develop."

Zoe and I were only too willing to take Dad's advice and drop the subject. All things considered, we would have to say that matters could be worse. *Snug* is not a word I would have thought I could use in this situation, but snug is how I felt at that moment in this stockade.

"Well, Dad, you sure called this one," Zoe said, stretching out on one of the mats, satisfied that Dad still had his power of prediction. "Supper in a few hours.... Hope it's something we can eat."

Dad nodded. "Well, there's always the MREs," he said. "But I'd like to save them as long as we have an alternative."

"There isn't much I wouldn't eat at this point, Dad," I said.

Feeling relieved and hopeful at finding these sailors, Dad stretched out on a mat. "I guess we're all pretty hungry," he said. "Looks like we got lucky. The good captain may be a little crazy, but I don't think he's dangerous." Dad was getting a look we had seen before. "Anyway, these are fine accommodations. I think I'll have a nap before dinner."

Dad often referred to the bear in everyone. "All a bear needs," he would say, "is a meal and a cave."

We could see the bear in Dad as he dozed off. Zoe had nothing more to say, and dozed off as well.

As I lay back, the captain's words echoed in my mind. *He thinks we're dead and waylaid in Limbo. There's no denying, our reality took a hard and sudden left the other day. Maybe the captain's on to something.*

I guess I blinked one time too many, because a nap took me by surprise.

"Let's eat!" Zoe said, nudging me out of some dream, back to the hooch we were calling home. "That's the dinner bell…, let's go!"

On the outside chance that the pirates might know something about them, I slipped poor Themi's satchel, which now contained our pictures as well as his bowl, over my shoulder, and followed behind my father and brother.

The setting sun brought on the eerie evening sounds of the jungle. The nocturnal chorus of screeches, growls, hisses, and roars was noticeably louder now than during the day.

The deep, soft sound of a foghorn was, in fact, a conch shell calling us to dinner. I was reminded of sunsets in Hawaii, where blowing the conch is a tradition.

"Wonder what's for supper," Dad said. "I'm starving! This will be a night to remember."

This remark jerked Zoe's head around. "Like last night wasn't?"

Zoe could always be counted on for two cents' worth of last word, which Dad and I usually let slide. However, these two cents set off the butterflies in my stomach—just in time to ruin dinner.

Ten steps brought us up to the sundeck of the captain's quarters. From there, we could see a partial view of the interior. The central fireplace radiated congeniality as its amber glow illuminated a long table like the one on the frigate. The primitive furnishings were graced with an opulence that spoke of other times and escapades. The table was set in silver with a plate of steaming meat, a bowl of breadfruit, two solid gold pitchers, and a basket of green apples. It looked like Thanksgiving.

A swimming feeling came over me as we approached the table and our hosts. It was another moment when life felt like a dream. The room threatened to dissolve as my eyes were met by men who claimed to be over one hundred years old and yet looked younger than Dad. I had to force my focus back toward the food in an effort to stabilize my thoughts.

The captain appeared out of the darkness and stood at his place. His four men were positioned on one side of the long table, and we stood across from them. As the captain took his seat, we all sat down.

He was more relaxed than in our last meeting. His eyes, while still penetrating, had lost their rage. Now a warm sense of adventure swept through me as we sat at the table together in the soft golden light of the fire.

"I am Captain Rosario," he announced, "and these men are my crew. Joaquin here is ship's carpenter.... Will Knox, who first spotted you out there in the bush, is our boatswain.... And Ben Wilkes and James Villa, able-bodied seamen both." His tone was that of a proud father. Each man nodded cordially as his name was mentioned.

"We're very honored to make the acquaintance of you and your men, Captain," Dad said. Then, not missing a beat, he introduced us, and we also nodded.

The simple introductions were more than sufficient to break the ice with these ageless pirates, who seemed eager to make our acquaintance. There was a warm feeling of positive potential afoot. After all their years here, I could only imagine to what extreme the boredom of their isolation had changed them.

To my surprise, we all ate in silence. At first, Dad, Zoe, and I felt awkward eating that way, but to our hosts this appeared to be totally normal. Our hunger must have been obvious as we devoured our food. The captain and crew took less and ate gingerly. The big bird tasted to me like rattlesnake. We had had rattlesnake once at a game dinner back home in Napa, and it tasted like chicken. This tasted like snake, but very tender. The breadfruit was tasteless, but the apples were like a gourmet dessert. After the meal, conversation resumed.

Putting down his mug, Rosario leaned forward. "How do you plan on spending your time here in Limbo?" he asked, directing his question to our captain. His curiosity expunged the torment from his normal expression.

Dad was quick to answer: "We sailed in and we mean to sail back out of here, Captain. We're seamen, like you…, although I'm sure we know very little, compared to the wisdom you have acquired. It's only been three years that we started sailing in California, where the Napa River flows behind the Paintball Jungle. As fate would have it, we have become able navigators." Dad's tone was upbeat.

Rosario glared at Dad as he said, "It will take more than your ability and my wisdom to ever leave *this* place!"

His wide-eyed expression, though relaxed, had never been completely absent. Now the conversation returned him to the original intensity of our first meeting. Once again, deep wrinkles appeared across that tormented forehead, and his lips tightened.

"Sail out of here, says you? We tried some time ago and failed. Lost a third of my crew…, eleven brave sailors, including a twelve-year-old cabin boy, all lost in that storm yonder. No one older than thirty, and that same broken boat washed back into this very lagoon. What message is in all of this? That we be prisoners, condemned to roam in the valley of death."

That jagged edge was returning to what had been an enjoyable evening. Dad looked at us, rolling his eyes. The boatswain stoked the failing amber embers to their full illumination as the captain continued to rant, staring into the flickering flames. His men listened, as we did, probably out of respect. I'm sure they had heard this monologue before. The captain was angry, crazy for sure, but not cruel. His men seemed to understand and accept him. The silence that followed was like a refreshing dessert.

When the captain fell quiet, sullenly gazing into the flames, Joaquin the carpenter picked up the tale.

"It was many years ago," he said, "when we made our first attempt to escape. We built two outriggers with sails. The second one is still intact, untried, sitting where we built it. The first one returned to this same lagoon, broken, battered, and with an unknown dead old black man lashed to the mast. After that, we have been unwilling to try again."

Time stood still as each ancient sailor told his tale. But all the while, the big picture remained elusive. This was truly the stuff of dreams. Here we were, somewhere between Never Neverland and Hell, listening to stories of plundering on the high seas. They told of their exploits with some other pirates from a place called Marauda.

"They were a ruthless bunch," Knox the boatswain said, "responsible for killin' most of our crew. We were runnin' from 'em when we were caught in the storm that marooned us 'ere. On that night, there were fifty-five of us aboard, along with an African cabin boy and a gypsy woman who was the cap'n's mistress."

"Ah, yes," Dad said. "We went aboard what's left of your ship in the lagoon. We saw two skeletons in the grand cabin."

"That's *her* skeleton on the bed," Joaquin said. "And the one at the table is Pizzo, the first mate. During the night of the storm, crazed with jealousy from discovering his young lover's secret affair with Pizzo, the captain poisoned her. Sparing her lover a fate worse than death, she poisoned him before the captain could take his revenge. Now Captain Rosario blames himself for bringing the temptress aboard and for the murders, which have condemned his crew to this timeless sentence on the island of the damned."

As these secrets were revealed to us, Rosario remained motionless, staring into the fire and showing no signs of objection aside from an occasional twitch in his right eye.

"But it wasn't that woman who drove the cap'n mad," Knox

said. "It was bein' swindled by the pirates of Marauda. They used 'im and our three ships to loot most of the treasure in the Caribbean, but then double-crossed us so that we lost two of our ships and most of our crew. Only our flagship, the *Tortuga*, escaped. The mask of madness that the cap'n now wears was caused by some 'orrible device he was exposed to by the ruthless Maraudians."

Dad, Zoe, and I were struck speechless. *Who were these pirates of Marauda?*

"Rosario's a good captain," Joaquin resumed. "He would take more treasure than lives whenever possible. There's a hold full of treasure from the *Tortuga Diablo*, which now sits on the bottom of the lagoon in ten feet of water."

Our eyebrows rose in unison as this particular was revealed.

"The wood from the ship," Joaquin explained, "was worth more to us than all those baubles. We realized that treasure had caused our predicament, and that it had no value in this place."

This thought struck a chord with us, and Dad nodded in agreement.

"It was the freshwater spring," Knox said, "that determined this site for the stockade. Safe 'ere behind these walls, our water is plentiful and risk-free. We spend our days tendin' our breadfruit crops and hikin' out to the great apple tree. In the evenin', we share our meals together."

The fire was stoked many times as we listened in silence to these men.

Finally, Dad asked, "Have you found any other wreckage

around here? Anything you could use as tools or weapons? Surely, there must be others who have washed upon these shores."

Joaquin shook his head. "Because of the titans," he said, "travel here is very limited. We've been attacked many times by the carnivores…, which is why there are only five of us left. It's been a long time since any of us have been down to the frigate. Not since we lost two of our party while offloading supplies."

It occurred to me that these men were more like monks than pirates in this Jurassic hermitage. It was obvious that the captain and crew were happy to see us come along. Whatever we had to offer would be a break in their monotonous imprisonment.

"Our main source o' meat," Knox said, "is the game bird we ate tonight. We lost one crewmember long ago, before we learned to protect ourselves from attack by the giant buzzards with the spikes ya see everywhere in the camp."

I told them of our encounter with these same types of birds earlier this morning at the blackberry bushes.

Villa chimed in, "They ain't very bright, those birds. We use a scarecrow on a rope. It's like fishing for birds, it is. Anytime we need fresh meat, we catch them easily. It's the simplest part of the whole ordeal…. Did you say blackberries, *hombre?*" He waited with baited breath.

I was amazed that after all their time here, they had never found the blackberries. "Yes, about an hour from here," I said, "there's a path, a game trail that leads back to a brook. It opens into a small clearing, and that's where the bush is."

That little tidbit had the undivided attention of the captain and crew.

"*Cielos!*" Villa said, salivating. "There's not much I wouldn't do for the taste of blackberries again!"

"Yeah, they were the best I ever tasted," Zoe said, rubbing it in.

These pirates had clearly been leading a limited existence, not knowing of the humungous berry bush that was so close, yet so far away.

Will Knox turned to us and asked, "What about you, mates? Let's 'ear *your* story."

The captain was still staring into the fire, but the boatswain's question had the other seamen waiting in hopeful anticipation.

Dad began: "You say you arrived here a hundred fifty years ago. That would be about 1850 or so, right?"

"No, mate," the boatswain answered. "July of 1818 it was when I last saw home."

"We last saw home about three months ago," said Dad, "and the year is 2006. I guess you could say we're from your future."

The room went still, with the crackling fire making the only sound during the moments it took for Dad's statement to sink in. We sat there together, face to face, with a paradox that lashed us unmercifully.

Villa broke the silence: "*Caramba!* I knew you weren't right.... I mean, I knew you weren't like us.... I mean—"

The captain cut him off. "The storm!" he cried. "It's that storm! It guides us as it binds us!"

No one reacted to this. Maybe it was because Rosario's rhet-
oric was nothing new to his men, or maybe the idea of us being
from their future had them captivated.

Joaquin took an apple from the basket and tossed it to me.

I caught the token from the smiling carpenter. It was a warm
gesture that dissolved the apprehension of the captain's rants
and restored the friendly atmosphere.

Wanting to hear more about us, Knox pressed on: "What's it
like, mate? What's it like?"

His face was lit up. Excitement and delight had finally come
to the stockade.

Dad smiled, looking into the old salt's eyes. Turning to Zoe,
he said, "Bring the shotgun and one of the two disposable flashlights."

Nodding, Zoe rushed off.

As Zoe slipped into the blue light of the moonless jungle, the
incessant cacophony was deafening, which probably motivated
him to move quickly.

Meanwhile, Dad continued his story. "I think you would
find the world we come from unrecognizable and awesome," he
said. "There have been many inventions since you last left port.
I hardly know where to begin. We now have ships that travel
unseen beneath the sea, which can sink or surface at will, and
ships that can fly higher and further than any bird."

At the mention of flying ships, the captain and his men started
to stir and mumble.

"We've seen ships that fly," the boatswain said, "long ago at sea, before we were marooned 'ere."

His words seemed incongruous, since there were no aircraft in the nineteenth century except for hot air balloons.

"Show them our pictures, Eli," Dad said.

I was already digging out the photos as he spoke. "Here they are," I said.

As I presented the Ziploc baggie containing the only proof of our discovery, the room was electrified with the buccaneers' awestruck reaction. First, it was the clear, pliable container that amazed them, and then it was the photos themselves. Dad explained that these were among the many new inventions from their future as he passed around the postcard size images. They looked at them long and hard before handing them back. Instead of asking questions about the saucer, they seemed to recognize it.

"The one we saw was also round," Rosario said, "but this is not the same one." He looked puzzled. "How are these pictures made? They're not drawings.... What are they?"

"They're called photographs," Dad said. "Pictures made with a device called a camera. Our time is full of such miraculous inventions. There are devices called radios that allow people to talk to each other over great distances as clearly as if they were in the same room."

At this point, the men had a vacant look from hearing about too many things they didn't understand. Little did they know, the show had just begun.

"I can only *tell* you about most of these things," Dad said.

"We lost our camera in the storm that brought us here. We were left with almost nothing after losing our ship. However, I can show you some of the things we were able to save."

As if he had lit a firecracker in their midst, Dad had refocused their attention. Casa Rosario was really rocking tonight, the atmosphere charged with delight and diversion. Even the captain seemed interested.

Just then, Zoe returned to our amber chamber of anticipation with the requested items. As he handed Dad the sawed-off shotgun, the men focused on it as if for the first time. Dad held it up so that the light could expose its design, similar at first glance to the pirates' own flintlock pistols, which was why Dad had chosen to start with it.

"This is called a shotgun," he began. "It shoots buckshot and reloads from the rear. Two barrels, not one…, and watch this." The gun seemed to break in half as Dad prepared to load it. "This shotgun is good for anything you need a gun for within twenty feet. It's loaded with these cartridges."

The amber light flickered brightly in the captain's quarters while the flames crackled and Dad tickled their amusement.

"Blimey, twenty feet ain't much of a range, is it?" Knox said. He had a point.

"This gun has a special purpose," Dad said, slipping the shells in and snapping the gun shut in one quick motion. "This will clear the room of undesirables without aiming." With that, he let the gun break in half again and removed the shells.

"Blimey, let's 'ave a look at it, then," said the boatswain.

"Never seen one that loads from the rear…, nor shot that looks like this."

Knowing what he was trying to say, Dad agreed: "After all, times haven't changed that much, have they? In your time as well as ours, such a specialized weapon is standard equipment aboard ship."

Captain Rosario went back to staring into the flames. The others were all gathered around Dad and his blunderbuss of the future.

"May I, sir?" asked the boatswain, his hand reaching to hold the wonderful weapon.

When Dad handed him the gun, Knox's eyes sparkled as he grasped it. Trying different positions, he held the piece naturally.

"Aye, 'tis a fine piece indeed."

Expecting it to break in half, Knox shook it slightly and looked at Dad with a puzzled expression.

"Like this," Dad said, flipping the lock lever, causing the gun to fold in Knox's hands. "Tomorrow, I'll show you what shooting it is like."

The crew hung on every word, waiting for Knox to let them have their turn. When he finally passed the gun to the others, they checked it out stem to stern. They also pored over the shells with fascination. When the shotgun came back to Dad, he set it down and smiled, for it was now time for his showstopper.

"This next thing represents one of the greatest achievements of mankind."

Once again, he had everyone's undivided attention, even the captain's. With no further ado, he whipped out the little red five-dollar disposable flashlight and flicked the switch. The beam of light shot out across the room into what had been darkness, revealing several muskets and barrels of shot and powder against the wall.

The men erupted in consternation, sounding like a chicken house with a fox in it. Their reaction spoke of terror, awe, and, of all things, recognition.

"It's *them*, Cap'n!" Knox exploded.

"They've found us!" Ben Wilkes said, speaking up for the first time this night.

"*Ay, caramba!*" Villa exclaimed. "It's the Maraudians!"

Rosario spun around to face his men: "Enough!" He took command of this moment of reactionary chaos as his men fell silent. "They are not the ones! Think back. Remember! They were different. These three have no idea of Terran and his bunch." Glassy eyes and sounds of agreement followed as Rosario concluded, "We'll say no more about it."

Taken aback by their reaction, we wondered what they were talking about. I imagined that their reaction had something to do with the treachery they had mentioned and the flying saucer they had seen. They thought that we might be the ones called the Maraudians. Whatever it was, the captain quelled their apprehension, and no more was said.

Pointing his finger, the captain asked, "What manner of lantern is this? What makes it so bright?"

Dad flicked the switch off, provoking a sigh of disappointment around the room. As best he could, he described the way light was made available from electricity, none of which they understood. He went on to explain that the flashlight wouldn't last long if we used it a lot. After another brief demonstration, the men agreed it would be best to save this wonderful tool for special purposes.

This last demonstration must have saturated their curiosity, for I had thought that there would be an endless stream of questions about life in the future, but this was not the case. Instead, everyone was still.

Dad finally broke the silence. "Captain," he said, "could we see the untried outrigger tomorrow, good sir?"

At this, the captain's brow contorted into a set of furrows that paralleled his eyebrows.

It was Joaquin who answered, "Aye, we'll show you the boat..., and you'll be welcome to it. But wherever you sail, it will be without us!"

Joaquin's declaration cleared the air for the captain, whose forehead immediately relaxed. Sensing that we had reached the limits of their attention, Dad picked up the shotgun and flashlight and gave us a nod, which meant *enough for now.*

"Captain Rosario," he said, "thank you for this excellent dinner and fellowship. However, it is late, sir, so with your kind permission, we will bid you and your fine crew a good evening."

Gazing back into the fire, the captain answered, "Good night, gentlemen."

The moon was on the rise now, making me wonder if that was why the denizens' chorus had subsided. Or perhaps it was because they had finished *their* dinner, too.

On the way back, Dad said, "The fact that they've been here so long without knowing about the blackberries speaks volumes about how sheltered these pirates have become."

"Yeah," said Zoe. "And what about their flying saucer stories? They weren't surprised…. They *recognized* it. And that flashlight really set them to thinking that we were the guys chasing them…. Hey, there's that beam we saw the other night."

He pointed to the top of the mountain. From this vantage point, it was obvious that the light was not coming from a town or resort.

"Man," said Zoe, "that's no spotlight, that's a beam…, like a laser beam!"

Our minds were racing, trying to make sense of what we were seeing. It didn't fit—a laser beam in the middle of a savage jungle!

Who or what could have such advanced technology?

"That beam," I said, "is clearly shooting out from the top of the mountain, and not from behind it."

"Maybe," Dad said, "it's what the hippie was talking about. Remember? He was waiting for someone to come and show him the way back home."

"We'll have to ask the captain about that," I said. "What was Themi trying to tell us…, something about a taboo on the mountain?"

"All I can remember," said Zoe, "is that he wasn't supposed to be there, and he was lost."

"Anyway," Dad said, "there's nothing we can do about it tonight. We'll have to take it up with the captain in the morning."

We watched the ominous red beam for another minute or two and then slipped into the hooch.

Lying there on my straw mat, I anticipated dreaming about dinosaurs, two-hundred-year-old pirates, and time standing still in a laser beam.

Like most mornings, I woke up before everyone else. These were my moments to think and meditate. By the time I finished sifting through last night's memories, Dad and Zoe were starting to stir, and I was thinking about the MREs.

"Hey, Dad," I called, holding up an unopened MRE, "whaddaya say we treat these dudes to some *real* food?"

After reaching into the sea bag and counting the MREs, he said, "Only fourteen packs left. I think we should save them in case we need 'em when we get outta here."

WHEN *we get outta here!*

Dad never even considered that we might be here for a hundred years.

"Do you have any idea," Zoe asked Dad, "how we'll be traveling that day?"

"I still think we're in the Bermuda Triangle," Dad said. "That's the only possibility that could even begin to explain what's going on here. But to answer your question, Zoe, we've gotta keep putting one foot in front of the other until it becomes clear how and when to make our move. Let's see what today will bring."

As we stepped outside, it was another radiant day in this paradisiacal hell. The compound already felt familiar and comforting. We were drawn by the strange but inviting smells of the fire pit, where one of the salts was tending a wok. With utensils ringing rhythmically, he had all the moves of a Benihana chef.

"What's for breakfast?" Zoe asked.

"If it's food you're after, mates," Villa said, "you've found it."

He smiled as he invited us to partake, pointing to some bowls that were laid out full and steaming. The food, which looked like hash, was the same flying snake we had eaten the night before, but this time well diced, flavored with something like licorice, and mixed in with breadfruit. This stuff tasted a lot better than the meal last night. We ate it all and thanked our chef for his great medley.

Now the other pirates began to stir about. Following the savory aroma of Villa's concoction, they soon joined us, and once again we were all together, except for Rosario.

"The captain will be wanting to see you," Villa said. "Watch for him to come down."

There was still no sign of Rosario when Joaquin stood up

and announced, "Today is apple day!"

"Every ten days or so," Villa explained to us, "we have to restock our apple supply. There's a huge tree not far from here, where the fruit is always ripe. We'll need all hands...some to pick, the rest to guard."

As Joaquin passed out side sacks to all of us, he asked Dad, "Do you still wanna see the outrigger today?"

"Yes, we do," Dad said. "Maybe we could use it. If we can't negotiate that pipeline to get out of here, we could at least explore what else there might be in this place.... Perhaps others have wrecked here like us."

This response perplexed the carpenter. "If there were other wrecks," he said, "what good would they be?"

"I have a theory about this place," Dad said with a smile. "If I'm right, we may find something we can use. There could be anything strewn up and down this beach. We might find just what we need to escape this place!"

The pirates' eyebrows rose with the thought of this possibility. There it was in a nutshell—Dad, the man with a plan.

But Joaquin wasn't convinced: "Like the captain said, you can go where you will, but we won't be making the cruise."

Hoping the answer might stir their dormant lust for adventure, Dad asked, "Have you explored this island at all in the time you've been here?"

The question exposed them. No longer were they sailors without a ship, they had become hermits without a cave. The idea of exploration had died long ago, and its rebirth brought blank expressions and slowly shaking heads.

"It's been at least a hundred years," Joaquin said at last, "since we lost the first three of our crew to the titans. We were stripping the wrecked frigate to build this fort when the first of the three was taken by a snake or eel that came out of the lagoon and snatched him from the dinghy he was offloading. The other two were devoured by a covey of titans near the outrigger shed."

His words had us riveted and thankful that our crossing of the lagoon had been uneventful. Hearing the accounts of their struggles to survive the many carnivores that were here, we began to understand their reluctance to venture too far from the stockade.

"After a while," Joaquin said, "we began to notice that none of us was getting any older."

I took the opportunity of this revelation to explore this paradox: "You say you came here over a hundred years ago, but no one has aged a day since then. How can it be that the sun rises and sets every day while time stands still?"

"This place is Limbo," Joaquin said.

As absurd as this sounded, I could think of no other possibility myself.

"The captain should be out and about soon," Joaquin said, and went off to do something. The others also got up and left for their hooches. For the moment, we were alone.

"No wonder these guys never leave home," Dad said. "You can live forever here if you just stay put."

He wasn't trying to be funny. Granted, it was understandable to resist being eaten alive at all cost, yet it didn't ease the reality of the alternative. This was a brutal life sentence, but the men's love of life had stifled their desire for adventure. It was inconceivable to us that anyone could go on like this, day after day. The pirates had their systems and routines; the stockade was clean and everything was shipshape. With only the occasional apple outings to look forward to, maybe this *was* Limbo, as Rosario and Joaquin had claimed. Or maybe this was Hell.

We were looking at the empty rack that the butchers had been working on when we arrived.

"Where do you think they store all that leftover bird?" I asked Dad.

Before he could answer, Captain Rosario came upon us from behind, catching us by surprise.

"They tell me you are determined to see the outrigger," he said, "so I will show it to you.... After that, you can assist us with the apples. The less time we're exposed, the better."

His wide-eyed expression was disquieting, but his congenial disposition allowed us to overlook it.

"Good morning, Captain," Dad said. "We'll be more than happy to help you with anything you need."

The captain turned to me and, pointing toward the cliff, explained, "We cannot have anything the titans will eat hanging around like bait. The beach is far below us. All remains are tossed over the side. The boatyard is this way. I'll take you there now."

"Please lead on, Captain," Dad said with a smile.

At that moment, Joaquin returned, wearing a cutlass and carrying one for the captain. Rosario's cutlass hanging at his side looked as natural on him as his pants.

Villa came up with two muskets, handing one to the captain.

"Don't be leaving that future musket behind, mate," Villa said to Zoe. "We'll probably need it before this day is over."

Will Knox arrived with two more muzzleloaders and blades for each of us. Dad strapped his cutlass on, but I declined. I wasn't going to leave my lucky axe behind. We both declined the pistols.

"We're not familiar with them," Dad explained. "We can learn about them later, but for now these blades will do."

I could tell from Dad's tone that he wasn't eager to master the ancient weapons. Zoe ran to our hooch to grab the shotgun, the first-aid kit, and the last box of shells from our dwindling supplies, and was back in a flash.

Leaving Ben Wilkes behind to guard the fort and close the gate behind us, we all slipped out into the jungle and picked up an overgrown foot trail.

In the daylight, the jungle was a very different beast. As we walked through the lush maze of vegetation, the hideous screeching of predators and saurian monsters was broken with moments of eerie silence. The pirates kept us at a quick pace and were constantly looking up and all around as we moved. They reminded me of nervous squirrels on the ground, away from the safety of their trees.

After a while, we came to a clearing with a large lean-to shed twenty feet long and fifteen feet wide. There she was, an authentic Polynesian-style outrigger, a real work of art, complete with eight paddles. Unlike any outrigger I had ever seen before, this one was equipped with a twelve-foot mast and sail. Gleaming in the late morning sun, the craft was stunningly beautiful. It was hard to believe that she was a hundred years old.

"She's a treasure, to be sure!" Dad said, beginning to sound a bit like a pirate himself. His eyes drifted as he imagined the potential of the lithe craft. Nodding to himself, he said, "This will do for a start."

Rosario smiled. "I haven't come here in a long time," he said. "I had forgotten how beautiful she is.... Your main problem, should you decide to sail her, will be the shortage of able-bodied oarsmen. You'll need at least six, and all you have is three."

Zoe and I looked at each other. Rosario's words had put a chill on the warm wave of hope we had been enjoying. But it was at times like this that Dad was at his best. He listened to the captain's rant with a determined smirk.

"You'll be going back to sea without us," Rosario said. "It's impossible to stay alive outside the fortress because the titans are everywhere. You'd be lucky to make your way to the beach, and then the surf...and then..., who knows what? You can stay here with us in Limbo and try to see how long you can last, or you can sail off and end it all. Not much of a choice."

The captain was about to enter that other place that he

inhabited, but then he caught himself and said no more.

"Aye, Captain, there doesn't seem to be," Dad said. He wasn't going to make any propositions while the captain was fired up, but I could see the wheels turning in his head, and hope was alive in his eyes.

"That's the way to the beach," Joaquin said, pointing to a downhill grade through dense undergrowth that led to the sand below. "We took the first boat down over logs to the beach, then dragged it out to the water. The swells split right and left there, making for a smooth ride out to sea between the breakers."

As Joaquin spoke, I could see Dad's face lighting up.

All this time, Rosario had said very little, staring out toward the sea.

Will Knox, though attentive, had not said a word all morning. This seemed odd to me, but what did I know about performing the same routine every day for a hundred years?

I guess these guys are in pretty good shape, all things considered.

"I bet," Dad said, trying once again to reignite the pirates' spirit of adventure, "there are all kinds of supplies and treasure from many time periods on this island. Just as our two groups are centuries apart, but wrecked within a half mile of each other, who knows what else we might find out there?"

As Dad laid it on just thick enough, Joaquin and Knox looked at each other. At the mention of treasure and supplies, I saw their eyebrows rise and fall. Dad saw it, too, and let his words settle on their imaginations.

The pirates were silent for the next few moments, while ideas of treasure and freedom raked over their synapses, reviving cravings that had been dormant for years.

Dad, the sly old farmer, had sown the seeds. But could he harvest the fruit?

The sun was directly overhead when Knox broke his silence: "Cap'n, it's gettin' on, and we 'ave another leg before turnin' back."

"Aye, we best be off for the apples," the captain said.

Joaquin and Knox took the point, followed by the captain, Villa, Dad, and me. Zoe brought up the rear.

The jungle sounds increased as we penetrated. I could identify a big cat not far away and a dinosaur, probably Big Bertha, echoing in the distance, as well as screeching and wings, *big* wings, unseen above the canopy. All this in the daytime proved to be as unsettling as the nighttime version, and we all assumed a higher state of vigilance as we hacked through an overgrown path that led toward the volcano's base.

"This is a long way to go, just for apples," I said to Knox.

"We've tried many times," he said, "to plant the seeds, but we've never been able to get even a sprout goin', so we finally gave up. I can't even guess why the apples are always ripe and ready."

After a while, we came to an open field. In the middle, there was the most magnificent and abundant apple tree I had ever seen, full of the same delicious green apples we had had for dessert the night before.

Rosario held up his hand, stopping us at the tree line. His men, like a SWAT team, entered the field and systematically checked out the skyline, treetops, and shaded areas. When they signaled to us, we approached the great tree.

"Start picking!" Rosario said to us.

While the pirates remained on vigil, Zoe slung his shotgun over his shoulder, climbed the accommodating tree trunk, and gathered apples from above us. Meanwhile, I laid my ax at the tree's base, next to where Dad was standing, and the two of us began picking the delicious fruit right from the ground.

What we didn't know was that there was a time limit. After a brief period of serious harvesting, the captain shouted, "Get ready to leave, mates!"

My sack was almost full as I hurried to gather the last few apples.

All at once, a piercing screech and large flapping wings signaled that we were under attack. This time there were five of them—the same kind of huge birds that had attacked us at the blackberries. Just like before, their intense downdraft engulfed us in a maelstrom as they knocked us down and came at us with talons and beaks. I could hear the other men yelling and cursing as Dad and I tumbled beneath the ambush.

With axe in hand, I rolled away and jumped to my feet, flailing to keep my attacker off me, but not connecting at all. The birds didn't see Zoe, who was in the apple tree about five feet above the bird that was pinning Dad down. Whipping the shotgun around to his grip, he pounced on the bird's back. As it reared its head away from Dad, Zoe pulled both triggers and rode the headless monster down as it crashed next to our dazed father. Zoe slammed two more shells in the chambers and ran over to where I was swinging my axe. As the giant bird screeched at me, Zoe executed it Mafia-style with two to the back of the head. Again, he reloaded and spun around to see what was next.

The shots from Joaquin, Villa, and Knox missed or failed to kill the birds. The captain hit his mark, but one shot is all you get with a musket. The four of them drew their cutlasses and proceeded to hack a wounded beast into a mass of feathers and goo as the last one flew away unscathed.

The immediate jungle had fallen silent from our commotion and had not yet resumed its hideous chant. Dad was in shock, bleeding from his head and neck. Although his wounds weren't serious, the lacerations needed stitches. The Krazy Glue in the first-aid kit would have to do.

"Make ready to leave," Rosario shouted. "We can't stay here any longer."

Obviously, we had to get out of there before the turkey buffet we had created was discovered. Fortunately, patching Dad up didn't take long. Zoe moved with the alacrity of a combat medic, closing the deep cuts one after another.

Next, we hastened to gather the apples that we dropped during the attack.

"Take all you can," the captain said, "and be quick about it, so this trip won't be wasted."

In a few minutes, we were on our way back to the compound,

with piercing, bloodcurdling roars ringing behind us. No sooner had we left the clearing than the first of the carnivores arrived to make its claim. We were spooked now and moving fast. With the Krazy Glue holding, Dad was able to keep up with the rest of us. The path from the apple tree back to the compound was well worn, compared to the one from the boat to the tree.

"We'll be there soon..., keep up the pace," the captain said, spurring us on.

As if to accent his words, a triumphant bellow blared over the deafening din, causing an abrupt pause in the clangor while the turkey dinner under the apples was claimed. Then the jungle momentarily fell silent again. Close calls were apparently a daily occurrence in this place. Today we were lucky, for the party was returning intact. At first sight of the stockade's double-thick tree trunk walls, we made a mad dash for the entry.

Ten yards from the fort, the carpenter called out, "Open the gate!"

Wilkes opened it and then slammed it shut as the last man ran through. A wave of relief came over us all. After that day, I had a new appreciation for apples.

The pirates were excited and impressed by Zoe's tactics, for he had no less than saved the day with his wonderful weapon.

Captain Rosario, however, was on another track. Before ascending to his quarters, he turned to Dad and asked, "And now that you've seen the outrigger and the price you've paid for apples, I'm curious..., are you still of a mind to go back to sea?" Glaring, he waited to hear what Dad would say.

Dad was haggard from the day's ordeal, but dauntless in his intentions. With his eyes piercing the captain's dreadful glare, he said: "My boys and I mean to leave this place, no matter what it takes, Captain. The boat's a beauty, but I don't think I'm ready to try that pipeline yet. I would like to use the boat to sail the coastline and search for better equipment. Where we come from, there's a place that fits the description of this island. It's called the Bermuda Triangle, where countless ships of sea and air have disappeared without a trace. I believe this is that part of the Bermuda Triangle where all those ships landed, just like we did."

Dad's words seemed to echo as he spoke.

The pirates were attentive as Dad confidently described his expectations. He had their attention and was bringing their imagination to a slow boil.

Even Rosario was in agreement, nodding his head. "Yes," he said, "we have heard of that legend. There might be something to it."

His men were encouraged by their captain's response.

Then Knox chimed in, "Aye, there may be all kinds of things lyin' about just waitin' to be discovered."

As we deposited the precious apples into several large baskets, the sun had another two hours left.

"We'll talk tonight at supper," Rosario said, dismissing us.

As the three of us returned to our hooch, I looked back and saw that all the men were following the captain up the stairs to his quarters. I would have loved to have been a fly on the wall and heard more about their impressions of the day's events.

Zoe gave Dad's cuts another gluing. We had done this before and knew that it worked well as long as the job wasn't too big.

Dad slept while Zoe and I tried to rest, but we couldn't doze. Before we knew it, the sun had set on another day full of challenge and the fight for survival. Although different from the daytime clangor, the raucous sounds of the jungle at night were every bit as unnerving.

When the conch called us to supper, it was almost dark. Dad woke up sore and stiff, but was able to walk with us to the big house. As we approached, we were surprised to hear laughter and loud voices emanating from above. Topping the stairs to the captain's quarters, a beckoning amber glow enhanced the exhilarating sounds from within.

Joaquin and Knox were waiting for us at the doorway. They seemed especially happy with Zoe. As we entered the room, Knox announced his arrival: "'Ere he is…Zoe, the flippin' bird-man 'imself!"

Joaquin put his arm around Zoe's shoulder as Knox continued: "You should've seen 'im, flyin' down on the titan as 'e blows its bloomin' 'ead clean off. Next thing, 'e's up and loaded and doin' it again."

The men were enjoying the retelling of the day's deeds, and the fact that they had a warrior from the future among them. Zoe smiled, humbly accepting their praise. As a champion paintball sportsman, who had to endure the boorish boasting of certain types of players, he knew better and was never one to expose himself to the pitfalls of hubris.

"Aye," said Knox, "a few more of those guns, and we'd be able to breathe around 'ere a lot easier."

The crew heaped praises on Zoe for a full five minutes.

Zoe smiled as he said, "Just the same, the next time we go for a walk, I think I'd like to have a cutlass on my belt, too!"

The men laughed and a bond started to develop among us all. Dad and I looked at each other and smiled, realizing that a new team was in the making.

The captain, who had been taking it all in, now assumed his place at the table. It was another round of big bird, the same as last night. We ate ravenously, hardly noticing the feral fowl's resemblance to snake. Everyone ate heartily, again without any conversation. Finally, when there was little food left, the apples were passed around.

A sullen shadow seemed to overtake Rosario's expression as he moved toward the fire pit where we were all now standing. Glowering at Dad, he grumbled, "Bermuda Triangle, says you..., Limbo, says I!"

To Dad, this was like asking for an encore, and he couldn't have been more delighted. "Maybe," he said, "they *are* one and the same, I don't know..., but that's my theory for now. If I'm right, there will be ships, boats, planes, weapons, and other forms of treasure. We could explore the coast with the outrigger and search for what we need to escape this place."

Each time the crew heard Dad tell the tales of the Triangle, they slipped under his spell more easily than before. He had the dormant sailors of fortune tossing in their sleep, tiring of slumber itself. From the seeds he had sown, Dad was reviving their lust for adventure.

The room was now charged with questions and speculation. Outside, the nocturnal clamor was dominating the evening as usual, but inside the fort, for the second night in as many days, the flames of excitement were thawing the ancient mariners' passion for action and treasure hunting. All things considered, Dad stood an excellent chance of offering them an alternative to their endless sentence in Limbo.

Our breakfast chef, Villa, chimed in, "One thing is sure..., boredom is our coffin, and these things you say are wondrous! That you are here with tools we've never seen speaks of the possibilities."

"Aye, mate," said Knox, "but it's the *impossibilities* that will get ya, ain't it? I'm not sure we could survive long enough to find these wondrous implements lyin' about amidst the titans. At least 'ere in the stockade, we can stay alive."

As Villa sat back to consider Knox's rejoinder, Dad responded: "I, for one, am not gonna sit around in a 'coffin of boredom,' as you call it. Survival has its limits. After a certain point, I would rather pass on to whatever awaits on the other side of this stagnant existence."

Rosario turned away from the flames and caught Dad's eyes in his own focused pools of perception. "Sitting in a coffin," he said bitterly, "is better than lying in one..., which is what will happen out there before very long. Those beasties today are the least of what you'll be coming across."

His tone was not threatening, but more matter-of-fact.

The men listened attentively as the two captains debated life and death.

"Aye, Captain, to be sure," said Dad, "travel can't be taken lightly..., but travel we must." Dad was beginning to pick up their style of speech. It sounded cool and was working. "If we plan carefully," he continued, "we should make the sea like the first boat did. Only this time we'll cruise the coastline, looking for what we need to make it back home. If you were to come and we all made it back, you and your men will have made a journey through time. When you think of it, it's the chance of a lifetime."

Dad was really rolling now. The pirates' eyes were wide, with their faces set in amazement. Possessing an uncanny knack for knowing when to quit, Dad let his words settle.

"We should all sleep now," the captain said, standing up to dismiss us. "There will be plenty of time to consider these things in the morning, but now I'm tired."

The path back to the hooch was dark on this moonless night, although, as usual, the sky was alive with shooting stars. The jungle echoed the insidious sounds of the savage carnage of this place, where nothing was safe from sudden extinction.

Once again, we noticed the beam shooting straight into the sky out of the mountaintop.

Joaquin, who was walking us back, said, "I've been seeing that light ever since I can remember, but I don't know what it is. It's like a rainbow.... It doesn't mean anything, it's just there."

All Dad said was, "Right," which really meant, *says you*.

As we stretched out, exhaustion overtook us. The constant stress of this place was taking its toll. Another day unlike any other had failed to stop us in our tracks. As we said good night, I noticed that we had formed a circle with our mats. That helped.

When Zoe woke up, he looked at Dad and said, "I really wanna get outta here."

Zoe was not a happy camper. His usual cool, calm, and collected self was being sorely tried.

Looking straight into Zoe's eyes, as he always did, Dad replied warmly: "I'm way ahead of you, son. First thing is, we need more crew to float the boat. That means we have to talk them into helping. We've gotta be careful and wait for the right time to say something that will change their minds. After that, we'll make preparations and get under way."

"Okay, Dad," Zoe said with a smile, "I think we've got them second-guessing about this place already."

Dad was an inspiration for positive action. Here we were in some twilight zone, and he had a way of making us feel like we were on nothing more than another family adventure. Although we were dealing with a few unexpected curves, we were still on the road that ultimately led home.

Reinflated, Zoe stood up, announcing, "I'm hungry!"

Dad smiled. "Let's go get some snake hash," he said.

As we came out of our hooch, the unmistakable sound of swords clashing came across the courtyard—swords clashing and men laughing. It was Wilkes and Villa fencing. Both men were displaying a certain ability and form. The captain and Joaquin were enjoying the match and the upbeat banter that went with it, while Knox was at the fire pit, preparing his version of breakfast.

"Alright, mates," Knox called. "Breakfast is ready, so 'ave at it!"

There was an alluring aroma in the air that was definitely not happening with yesterday's concoction. This hash was a lot better tasting than Villa's, and the atmosphere was upbeat and lighthearted.

When we finished eating, Rosario looked at Dad with a smile. "We've had a change of heart," he said.

That caught us by surprise. Even the jungle clamor seemed to fade out.

What's he saying?

The captain's smile changed back to the usual grimace. "That is," he added, "*some* of us have changed our minds about going on the voyage you proposed last night.... Will Knox, James Villa, and Ben Wilkes want to search for the things you say should be found strewn about...or at least to have another adventure and taste the thrill of life again."

We couldn't believe our ears. Dad's pitch last night had sparked a new hope in them. Or maybe they had decided to just go for broke. Whatever it was, we were over the first hurdle. Dad winked at Zoe.

"Joaquin and I," continued the captain, "will stay here and wait until such time when you return with the means to make our getaway."

Dad's work was done before he knew it. His eyes twinkled as he saw his plan taking shape.

The captain's new optimism infused the whole idea with a confidence that made it all seem possible. Pointing down toward the beach, he said, "We'll reclaim the path to the sea, and Joaquin will make sure the boat is still sound. Then we'll smoke the meat and bring a load of apples. Not much room for supplies on that rig, but we'll make do."

Rosario was alive with the idea he was presenting. I thought he would be forbidding. Instead, he had embraced Dad's plan even though it meant he would be three crewmen lighter.

Zoe was anxious about his luggage. "Aye, Captain," he said, "we'll take our gun, a fishing pole, and a spear."

Rosario shot a fiery glare at Zoe. "You can leave your fishing pole here," he said. "You're the smallest things in that sea, to be sure."

That was not what Zoe wanted to hear.

Joaquin added, "Aye, and the spear will only be getting in the way as well."

Dad nodded in silent agreement.

The captain sighed. "It won't be the first time," he said, "that treasure was found by following a madman's tale."

Dad stopped Rosario as he started to rant. "Madman, maybe,"

he said, "but the Bermuda Triangle was a real part of the world we came from, with hundreds of ships that were lost without a trace. To remain here may provide safety, but not enough. By venturing out, we stand an excellent chance of finding other vessels or some usable salvage. If this is to be our final voyage, so be it. I thought our last cruise would be our final one. Although my boys and I embrace life and all its potential, we ultimately do not fear death. We believe life goes on, and so will we."

Dad's philosophy was familiar to us, and we knew he was always ready to apply it wherever the rubber met the road.

Rosario understood Dad. This point had been made in slightly different terms in last night's talk with his crew. One thing we all had in common was the epiphany produced by the total submission to the forces of nature. "Here today and gone tomorrow and back again," as Dad would say.

Ever the boatswain, Knox was now absorbed in estimating and prioritizing our needs for the task at hand. "We'll be needin' powder," he said, "'bout twenty barrels, I'd say."

He had the picture: first things first.

I wondered what we would need twenty barrels of powder for, but I kept silent. The way the men were responding inspired my confidence.

With his cutlass belted and his musket in hand, Joaquin announced his intentions: "I'll go down to the outrigger and start getting her ready."

He was off as Knox, Villa, and Wilkes armed themselves and prepared to go down to the lagoon.

"We'll help with the powder if you'd like," Dad said, looking at one of the cutlasses that remained unclaimed.

Noticing how Dad was admiring the scabbard, Knox said, placing it in Dad's hands, "Help yourselves to the side arms. Wear them in good health."

Zoe's eyebrows rose as he scanned the area for "side arms."

Dad, who was buckling the antique scabbard and belt to fit snugly, said, "He means *these*."

"Thanks," Zoe said, setting down his shotgun, and strapping on a cutlass of his own.

I also took one from the pile.

Halfway up the stairs, Rosario turned back to us. "And may we all share dinner together this evening," he said. That was his way of saying *good luck and nice chatting with you*.

Knox called out, "Let's go!"

Dad was eager, looking a bit like a buccaneer himself, with a cutlass on his belt and a gleam in his eye. We followed Knox and the others out of the fort.

As we closed the gate behind us, the fierce pitch of the feral clamor injected us with apprehension. Nevertheless, the steady descent kept us focused on our footing. Otherwise, the savage sounds of the jungle would have unnerved us. The incessant hissing and screeching made the unseen dangers feel all the more imminent. It was a long ten minutes before we got to the bottom of the steep path that led down to the lagoon.

Wanting to offload as quickly as possible, Knox pressed his men as they lowered an ancient lifeboat down out of the lush canopy.

"Open ground is a constant danger," he said, pointing into the boat. "This powder will give us an edge if we get surprised."

"Something tells me," Zoe cracked, "that it's *when* we get surprised, not *if.*"

Knox grinned. "Aye!"

After unwrapping a barrel of black powder from its oilcloth protector and leaving it at the trailhead, we proceeded to drag the boat twenty yards to the lagoon.

"Zoe and Ben," Knox commanded, "you stand guard while the rest of us do the job."

With each of us taking an oar, we reached the *Tortuga Diablo* in minutes. After posting a second barrel ten yards back toward the tree line, Zoe and Ben watched us and waited. Knox tied off the lifeboat as we climbed aboard the frigate.

The mood of the buccaneers changed the moment we got aboard. I imagined they were immersed in bad memories. It was different for us as well. Now that we knew about the ship's past, she really seemed haunted, complete with skeletons and probably ghosts. With never even a look in the direction of the grand cabin, Knox passed the captain's doors and descended to the powder magazine. He was focused and deliberate in his moves as he separated the first barrels from the main supply and rolled them our way. I admired his ability to work so efficiently when it was clear he was spooked.

With little conversation, we wrestled twelve barrels into the lifeboat on the first trip and twelve more on the second. From the lagoon to the boat launch was a half-mile walk just inside the canopy. After we piled eighteen barrels under a cover of palms, Knox immediately started back.

"We'll set this up later," he said. "Let's be off."

After we returned to the lagoon, we put the lifeboat back up into the trees and then inched our way up the steep grade through the undergrowth to Casa Rosario, with each of us carrying a barrel of powder strapped on like a backpack.

Suddenly, we became aware of the absence of the usual clamor. The abrupt silence paralyzed us, causing the hairs on the back of my neck to stand erect.

"*Jee*-zus!" Dad said, sounding his alarm.

"*GRMPH!*"

This came from below. I didn't want to look as I turned around.

"Godzilla!" Zoe quipped—always a bad sign.

"*GRMPH!*"

It was a titan, some kind of Jurassic gargantuan, maybe sixty yards behind us and about to discover our presence. Its scaly green head had two large horns above bulging eyes. At least fifteen feet high at the hip, it was bent over, sniffing the powder keg we had left behind at the trailhead.

I don't think any of us knew the specific names of the many types of "titans," as Rosario called them. Raptors, dinosaurs, whatever— the bottom line was that they came in all sizes, ranging from large to humungous, and they were always popping up, trying to end our days.

Without hesitation, the buccaneers raised their muskets, took aim, and fired in unison at the powder keg

Crack—Boom—Boom—Crack—Boom!

BABOOM!

In spite of the horrific explosion, the monster remained standing, but lost interest in our seductive scent and staggered off in another direction. The ripping explosion added man's roar to the savage cacophony, to which the jungle paid its respect with a moment of utter silence.

When we arrived at the top of the hill, the captain and Joaquin stood armed and ready.

"All accounted for, Cap'n," Knox called ahead. "It was a snapper..., but 'e's gone now."

The jungle had reclaimed the ancient path from the outrigger down to the sea. Working diligently into the early evening gave us a considerable start on what must be done before we would be ready to haul the boat to the beach. The day's accomplishments consoled us as we scurried back to the stockade. It was going to be dark in an hour, and we were tired and hungry. We didn't talk about the nightmarish edge that every moment held. Instead, we just kept thinking about the next step in our plan to get home.

That night, Joaquin told us how he had come across a big bird's nest that contained an egg. His description of stealing the egg and getting the watermelon size sphere home in one piece furnished some very welcome comic relief.

Knox changed Joaquin's trophy of the day into an omelet concoction that was darn near tasty, and the only time there was no conversation was while we were eating.

After supper, the captain said, "Based on what you got done today, the preparations for your departure shouldn't take more than two more days. Except for needing a new sail, the outrigger is ready. All that's left to do is reclaim the boat path to the beach."

"Agreed, sir," Dad said. "Tomorrow's another day.... And now we best be getting to sleep."

By the time we reached our hooch, we were dead tired. Even so, we stood for a few minutes, contemplating the red beam that we saw every night.

"Man," Zoe said, almost talking in his sleep, "I sure would like to know what's up with that."

"Maybe," I answered, "maybe we don't *wanna* know."

Dad interjected, "Tomorrow's waiting, boys, let's get some shuteye."

When excitement is your alarm clock, you're asleep one moment and the next instant wide awake, with a jagged current of anticipation shooting through to your core.

"There's a lot of work to do before we can launch," Dad said, as if we were in mid-conversation. "No use worrying about what comes next until then."

"I don't want us to end up stuck here, that's for sure," Zoe said, jumping to his feet.

Referring to his way of praying, Dad replied, "We need to visualize things turning out better than we can imagine."

We never actually saw or heard Dad pray, but he often referred to his successful communications with the Great Spirit with all the enthusiasm of a master chef revealing his ingredients.

We were feeling rested and upbeat, ready for another day of heavy labor. The smell of breakfast was in the air as we joined the others. Another round of Joaquin's omelet was the morning special.

I was thinking of those MREs stashed away like Christmas presents in July when the captain broke my reverie.

"If we can make the path ready today," he said, "you can be away by tomorrow."

"Aye, Cap'n, the sooner, the better," Knox answered, walking toward the powder kegs. "We'll need to bring along four more kegs. We don't wanna be caught off guard."

The first thing we did upon arriving at the boatyard was hoist four barrels into the trees, fifteen feet above the ground, one dangling at each corner of the perimeter. We did this systematically, with little direction from Knox. Dad and Rosario stood guard while the rest of us finished reclaiming the old path that was to be our runway to the beach below. We worked undisturbed for several hours, making steady progress using machetes to cut our way through the brush, and taking turns with the axe whenever we came upon a tree.

By the time we were halfway down to the beach, we had felled several trees, which allowed broad shafts of golden light to pierce the canopy, expunging the somber shade that remained everywhere else.

In the midst of our work, we were startled by a double report and explosion. The jungle din had not yet regained its momentum as we all ran back up to the top. Dad and Rosario were waiting as we reached the yard. Behind them, one of the four trees holding the powder kegs was now reduced to what looked like a giant smoldering matchstick.

"A couple more big birds," said Rosario, scanning the treetops as he spoke. "They thought they'd have another go at us, but we changed their course midflight. They know we're here now."

We took a break under the canopy. Villa passed around a water flask and pieces of snake jerky, sea-salted and not that bad.

"Once we're under way," Villa said, "this is what we'll be eating till we find something else."

His comment produced an expression of disgust on Zoe's face. But, in a rare moment for him, my brother remained silent.

With four hours still left before sunset, we were determined to cut through to the beach. Slashing the brush away and chopping trees was a laborious task, but the camaraderie with these ancient buccaneers made the work enjoyable, providing some diversion from the constant anxiety of the savage environment.

"That barrel-on-a-rope trick works well," I said to Joaquin.

"Aye, but we'll run out of powder one day."

"*There's* a pleasant thought," Zoe cracked as he chopped away at the last ten feet of undergrowth.

Finally, after hacking and whacking everything left in our way, we were at the beach, near the powder stash. As the sun started its downward tilt, we looked back at the path we had cleared, which was twelve feet wide and a quarter-mile long. From where we stood, it looked like the boat would slide down to the beach on its own.

Worried that the boat was too heavy, Knox said: "We 'ad more 'elp the last time we dragged one of those down 'ere. Sure, it'll be easy goin' down alright.... It's when we reach the sand that I'm worryin' 'bout."

I could tell that Dad wished Knox had kept his pessimism to himself. "It's a hindrance to getting things done," I'd often heard him say.

But then he said aloud, "Where there's a will, there's a way."

For the moment, his cliché seemed to plug the latest hole in our confidence.

With that we fell silent and started back to Casa Rosario, tired and hungry. It was almost dark as we closed the gate behind us. The mood of the group was now at a low point. The combination of hunger and fatigue, along with the unknown factors of the adventure on which we were about to embark, resulted in a decline in our morale.

Once again it was time for Dad's magic to relight the fires of enthusiasm.

"All hands, now hear this!" he cried. Catching us by surprise, his words spun us around, shaking off our melancholy. "Tonight, my friends, we'll sleep with a good hot meal to bring us luck and to introduce you to the food of the future!"

Dad was becoming a regular source of amazement to these guys.

"What are ye saying, man?" Rosario asked with a raised eyebrow.

Knox and the others were eager to see what Dad had in his bag of tricks this time.

"Prepare yourselves," he said. "In ten minutes, we'll meet and eat."

That was all Dad would say. Of course, *we* knew what he meant, but we weren't going to spoil the surprise. Dad always knew how to use what he had. In the time it took to retrieve the MREs and join the others in the captain's quarters, Dad had transformed the men's mood from tired and pensive to stirring anticipation.

As he distributed the MREs marked "Captain's Country Chicken," it was the shiny printed foil that first captured the pirates' amazement.

Ignoring their questions about it for the moment, Dad started his demonstration, issuing directions to the men as he went. As they followed along, the crew reminded me of curious monkeys, clicking and chuckling with delight over every detail. When we poured water in and the MREs started to heat up, a look of panic and amazement came over them. But they were delighted as we went through the dining experience.

The evening took on a rosy hue as the day's accomplishments and the meal from the future had everyone feeling the potential in our plans once again. The captain was more like a brother with his men than usual, I thought.

After a while, the talk went back to the project at hand.

"Still," Knox said, "the boat may be too 'eavy for the eight of us to drag across the sand to the water."

"I think," Joaquin said, "if we cut some poles, we could use 'em to help us roll the boat over the sand."

Things were cooking now. The pirates' high energy was stimulating an unstoppable surge of optimism among us all. We would sleep well tonight.

On our walk back to the hooch, Zoe said, "One more day..., maybe two at the most..., and we'll be outta here."

As usual, the shooting stars were in abundance. But it was the massive sable cone-shaped silhouette of the mountain that demanded our attention.

"There it is," I said.

The inscrutable red beam with its puzzling purpose projected out of the ominous pinnacle into the boundless starlit regions of space. It never moved or made any sound, but was always there, night after night.

Inside the hooch, we stretched out on our mats, exhausted but content. Hope was alive as a blanket of confidence covered our vulnerability for the night.

"Dad," Zoe asked, "can we eat the rest of the MREs

tomorrow?"

"Goodnight, fellas," was his only response.

When I awoke in the morning, it was raining. The penetrating downpour made the little hooch feel cozy. However, the warm feelings of last night's fellowship were gone. The confidence that had so snugly tucked us in was as absent as the sunshine on this stormy dawn.

Our tenuous situation had me feeling apprehensive about everything. The impending outrigger trip was an intrepid plan, though questionable at best.

Zoe was awake and on the same track, his first words echoing my own thoughts. "I'm not so crazy," he said, "about that outrigger plan today. Maybe we should check out that laser beam before we go back to sea."

Outside, the gentle downpour became a torrential onslaught as Dad continued sleeping, oblivious to the horrendous pummeling that made it difficult to hear anything else. I imagined that if it kept up like this, our only problem would be *reaching* the outrigger, not launching it.

Raising his voice, Zoe continued, "Who knows what we might find up there?" His words, which began to take on a life of their own, made me feel their double edge. "Anyway," he said, staring at the rain, "we would still be on land. We're gonna miss stretching out on these mats if we have to sleep on that rig."

Zoe had a way of weaving words into the imagination. Phantom cramps sprinted through my body as he spoke.

An accelerated final downpour brought sun and rainbows on its heels, as if to remind us natives of Limbo what heaven might look like.

Casa Rosario was built on a terrace overlooking the sea. In the morning sun, silhouettes of pterodactyls dotted the horizon, which was resplendent with a radiant rainbow arching over aqua swells emanating from the distant pipeline. Taking in this surreal view, I was reminded in no uncertain terms that our plan for the journey back home did not ensure escaping this Jurassic existence. The fact that we all had sailed in was the hope, if not the premise, that we could sail back out. I decided to keep these thoughts to myself. Debating them could only bring unwelcome answers.

"The laser beam's off again," Zoe said.

"Only comes on at night," I answered. "Trouble is, climbing that mountain might be impossible. I wonder how difficult making our way through to that volcano would be. And climbing that giant traffic cone doesn't appear doable from here."

Zoe nodded. "Yeah," he said. "Laser beams and dinosaurs..., what a place!"

By now, Dad was waking up, and Zoe started right in on him.

"We were thinking, Dad," he said, "maybe we should check out that mountain laser beam before we go to sea."

"Yeah, while we're still here on land," I added. "Maybe there are answers up there."

Dad considered our words. "Maybe we *should* check it out," he said. "It wouldn't hurt to put off the launch a couple more days."

Dad always listened to whatever we came up with.

"On the other hand," he said, "maybe we should go looking for salvage first to upgrade our equipment."

"Yeah," Zoe said. "Our weapons aren't very formidable right now."

"The outrigger's our strongest asset for putting our escape package together," Dad continued. "The main thing is that we need to stay focused once we decide what we're gonna do."

Zoe and I nodded.

"I'll tell you what," Dad concluded. "We'll finish the launch preparation while we think about it. We can decide later."

"Works for me," I said.

"Me, too," said Zoe.

Then we headed off to the breakfast club. As usual, exposure to Dad dissipated all things pessimistic for us. Gone were the early morning anxieties. We were ready for whatever was coming. Somehow, the torrential downpour and subsequent sunshine provided an inspirational feeling of renewed potential for what lay ahead.

Today's plans called for the placement of powder kegs at strategic points in trees and on the beach. That was the easy part. We would need at least a dozen ten-foot poles to help roll the boat over the sand.

"Once we're all out on the sand with the outrigger," Rosario warned, "the powder will be our only chance if those birds spot us."

Before we all left the fort, Will Knox gave the three of us a quick but thorough lesson in loading, aiming, and firing a flint-lock rifle. We loaded and fired a half dozen times. Aiming and pulling the trigger as a firecracker goes off inches from your eye while holding your bead takes getting used to. Zoe caught on after the first try. By the fourth round, we were all able to do the deed. Knox had an easy way about him, which made learning to load and shoot a pleasant experience.

"You'll need to know what to do when the time comes," he said.

His remark earned one of Zoe's side-glance quips: "Yeah, you mean if you have *time* when the time comes."

Knox smiled at Zoe's savvy. "Aye," he said, "you'll do.... Let's be off."

We joined the others and started out. Zoe carried the rifle and slung the shotgun over his shoulder.

"Only thirty-five shells left," he said.

His inventory was unsettling because it was devoid of sarcasm. He was not happy about the prospect of running out of shotgun shells, because the flintlocks left much to be desired.

The quarter-mile path of cleared jungle, which represented a lot of sweat and sore muscles, was a sharp contrast to the dense foliage that surrounded it. Our efforts would be rewarded when it was time to move the boat.

We spent the morning looking for suitable trees to cut into rolling poles. At lunch break, when Dad asked the captain about the beam we saw coming out of the mountain at night, those familiar four rows of wrinkles furrowed his brow.

"That be the Rapture," he said. "One way out of here, to be sure!"

It was evident that Dad had struck a nerve on Rosario's darker side. Zoe and I exchanged glances, as if to say, "Here we go again." We braced for another rant from the half-mad pirate captain.

"'Tis the stairway 'tween glory and the fiery brimstone," he said. "Years ago, three of our party set out to find the Rapture and were never seen again."

That was enough explaining for Dad. He would draw his own conclusions anyway. "We're burning daylight!" he said. Everyone looked at him. "Time's a wasting, and there's still much to do."

Amidst grunts and agreements, we resumed our efforts as Dad and the captain stood watch at the top of the hill. Knox and the other men cut the selected trees into poles, and Zoe and I carried them down to the tree line.

Work was moving at a steady pace when a stunning silence replaced the background clamor of the denizens' perpetual chorus. I looked at Zoe, acknowledging the change, when, almost unnoticeably but then very definitely, the ground started shaking. We knew what that meant.

The crew did, too. Dropping their tools and weapons, they

ran across the clear cut into the jungle and scrambled up the tall trees. Zoe and I took cover under an ancient fallen tree trunk and ferns. Since there was no time to try to make the tree line, this would have to do. Zoe and I huddled together, holding our breath as the tremors intensified and the stampede came closer.

Boom! Boom! Boom!

"Here they come!" Zoe whispered, ducking lower as he spoke.

They appeared halfway up the clear cut. Popping out of the perimeter, they stood still for a moment, considering the potential of this new exit route. At least fifteen feet tall, they had long thick tails, large powerful hind legs, and shorter forelegs with clawlike talons. They were hideous, with large, dirty brown, red-tipped scales and greenish-white underbellies. Mouths gaping and drooling, spiked teeth glistening, their lizard heads looked all around as their incessant guttural hissing emphasized their every move. The mini-earthquakes continued even though they stood still, considering their options.

The group of five had just started down the clear cut toward our position when Big Bertha, our "friend" from the other day, came out hot on their heels. A much larger dinosaur, she stood at least twenty-five feet high and was moving as fast as her smaller prey. Bertha took a hard right into the clear cut as if it had always been there. As we watched in horror, the ground thumped us windless. No doubt about it, the stampede was coming straight at us. The sounds of wood splitting and crackling like timber on fire reverberated as the covey of terrorized lizards sought escape from their relentless predator.

Sheer terror paralyzed us. If these creatures were inclined to snatch us from our burrow beneath the overturned bole, we would be helpless to prevent it, and our lives would be over.

The desperate herd came by us and over us. The thunderous impact of their hooves made our extinction an imminent possibility as we tried to brace against being bounced out from under our cover. As one of them jumped over our hiding place, I was certain for a split second that it saw me. Our eyes locked on each other for a moment as the creature bounded over us.

Bertha came straight down the path and took another hard right when she reached the sand. The Jurassic menace had inadvertently saved us from extinction, since her prey were forced to pass us up and flee for their own lives. What we felt was more than relief as they took their problems elsewhere. We couldn't believe we were still intact.

"By the look of things," Zoe said, "she'll have one caught before too much longer."

"Better them than us," I said. "Let's go!"

Shocked and shaken, we climbed out from under the ancient tree trunk. The jungle noise was still absent in the wake of the rampage. The tremors subsided as abruptly as they had started.

Making our way back up toward Dad and Rosario, we were joined by Knox and his tree climbers. The men were spooked, but realizing that we had all survived the melee, they regained their confidence.

"*There* was a bit of excitement," said Villa, red-faced. "All that fuss and not a shot fired."

He was trying to make light of the fact that if they hadn't been preoccupied with Big Bertha, the raptors would have ended our days before settling any gripes they had amongst themselves.

Knox spurred us on. "Let's not press our luck," he said.

The showdown on the beach was not over yet, as evidenced by the ghastly racket that billowed through the canopy.

"The work is done for now," Villa said. "I don't think we would have finished today anyway. They'll be back, and we best be gone. Tomorrow, we'll move the boat down to the beach and get some rest before we shove off the next morning."

We couldn't have agreed more as we started up the hill. Dad and Rosario, standing at the top, had seen everything and concurred that our launch path secret was out. As we hastened back to the fort, its relative safety, in the light of Big Bertha, now felt like a turtleneck sweater in a nudist colony.

Joaquin rustled up the quickest batch of snake hash yet, and we all devoured it.

After supper, we made plans to finish the work by tomorrow and be off after resting a day or so. Dad did not bring up the "Rapture beam," and nothing more was said about it. Rosario told us again that he and Joaquin would help to see us off, but he, for one, was not yet ready for the final voyage. It had been a long day, and everyone was ready for sleep.

Back at the hooch, Dad, Zoe, and I sat in a circle in the center, as we often did, and resumed the morning's discussion.

"I don't know, guys," Dad began, "it seems pretty dangerous

to tackle the mountain. Maybe we'd better take our chances and get back out to sea. Those snappers were occupied with their own problems today, but they were on you before you knew it. Considering what we've seen, I'd say we've been lucky so far, and I don't wanna push it."

We stretched out for the night in silent agreement. The choices weren't great anyway. We'd better forget about climbing a mountain full of things that were trying to eat us. I was depending on Zoe's defense mechanism, jokes in the face of terror, to pull me through this night, but he was already out.

How does he do that?

The nightmares were lining up outside, waiting for me to close my eyes. Unthinkable images of seeing my father and brother chewed up and gulped down like pieces of chicken were forcing their way in, keeping sleep almost out of reach.

In the morning, we were amazed at how soundly we had slept, but decided not to waste any more time than was necessary to escape this place. After yesterday's encounter with the giant reptiles, the idea of exploring the mountain was on the back burner once again. Our decision had been made for us — we would leave as soon as possible.

After breakfast, we completed the pole project without a hitch. Finally, it was time to move the boat down to the beach. The downgrade allowed us to guide the craft to the edge of the sand without any trouble. By now, it was mid-afternoon and time to return to the fort. Leaving the outrigger on the beach at the tree line felt risky, but that couldn't be helped. Short of Big Bertha coming along and stepping on the boat, it should be okay for one night.

Tomorrow, the last stretch through the sand would be a challenge, although Joaquin's method of rolling poles should do the trick. We would bring the three barrels of supplies and be off to our next stop in this seemingly endless dream that was our life. For better or worse, this night would be our last at Rosario's dinner table.

The atmosphere was tentative as we made our way back to Casa Rosario. It was obvious that the men were wrestling with their decision to quit this endless monotony and go for broke. They seemed excited about the adventure one minute and reflective the next. Rosario and Joaquin were more subdued than usual. Understandable, I thought. As we got back to the fort, I wondered what Rosario's *bon voyage* speech would be like.

When we passed the captain's quarters, Knox and Wilkes began assembling our meager provisions at the foot of the stairs. The sparse supplies spoke of the perilous trek we were about to undertake.

Back at our hooch, Dad, Zoe, and I collapsed to rest, but couldn't sleep.

"Three barrels, two filled with water," said Zoe, "the third with snake jerky and apples." He was obviously not a happy camper. "No powder, just swords." Then, placing the shotgun next to the side sack he had inherited from Themi, he said, "Well, I'm not leaving *this* behind."

As he had done many times before, he opened the sack and slipped the bowl out to examine it. It was a simple bowl, a bit pointy, with symbols around it and what looked like a ruby in its center.

As he examined the dead hippie's bowl, he said, "I think that laser beam, the mountain, and poor Themi are all part of the same intricate puzzle. Themi used this to drink. I wonder if it has any other purpose. And what are these symbols all about?"

After a moment, he returned the bowl to the sack.

As usual, we joined the pirates for dinner. The mood was somber this night, as we all anticipated our desperate plan. Once again, morale had to be rescued from new depths by Dad's impeccable timing as he brought out the last of the MREs.

"I'll miss you, that's for sure," said Rosario. "I must confess, a part of me wants to go with you."

"You won't change your mind, Captain?" Dad asked. "There's room in the boat.

Rosario shook his head.

"Well, then," Dad said, "thank you for your hospitality. Please accept this flashlight as a token of our gratitude."

Delighted to accept the wondrous object, Rosario flicked the side switch and pointed into the darkness, panning across the room. He repeated this every few minutes, each time the crew reacting as if they were watching a movie.

The MREs and the lightshow served Dad's purpose. He had

us alive again and excited about what we might find and what we might do.

As we walked back to the hooch with our spirits restored, we chuckled as Dad recreated the animated images of the captain.

"Maybe I should have given him *both* flashlights," he said. "Judging from the light show he gave us tonight, he'll burn that one out in no time."

We laughed at Dad's remark until we saw the beam again and fell silent. When we arrived back at the hooch, we were exhausted as usual.

Before going to sleep, Dad handed the remaining flashlight to Zoe. "Put this with the shells," he said. "They'll both need to be kept dry."

Stretched out on my mat, waiting for sleep, I wondered what Themi's people were doing and what else was going on inside the mountain with that laser beam.

III

Once again, the day's exhaustion was expunged by a deep, dreamless sleep. It was a morning like no other. As we walked to breakfast, I took in the interior of the stockade for what would probably be the last time. I wondered what sleeping would be like tonight and if we would regret relinquishing Casa Rosario's relative security for the chance of escape. On balance, the latter was still more desirable.

The captain and crew had finished breakfast by the time we joined them.

"Top of the mornin', mates!" called Knox. "Get yourselves some vittles, and we'll be on to doin' that which is left to do." As he greeted us, he handed us steaming bowls of snake hash.

Rosario was standing by, inspecting his flintlock.

"We should be away by early this afternoon," said Dad, "unless there's a hitch. What say you, Captain?"

Rosario finished with his rifle and set it down before replying, "But there's *always* a hitch."

His comment reignited the flames of apprehension within us as we all headed for the beach. Constant butterflies in the stomach were part of the normal way of life here, but on this morning that metaphor fell short. It was more like terrified butterflies, a feeling that threatened to turn our legs into rubber. We dreaded thinking too far ahead, so we just put one foot in front of the other, carrying out our desperate plan in the belief that we would escape our predicament. But our strategy flew in the face of the fact that it was just another day in the endless stagnation of this feral morass, which threatened our extinction at every juncture.

I wonder if we haven't rationalized ourselves into pure madness.

We placed the last powder kegs at the midway point between the jungle and the beach. From there it was only fifty yards to the water. At last, everything was ready.

Each man took hold of the outrigger and waited for the word. This life in Limbo was nerve-wracking, and the venture we were about to embark upon was every bit as intimidating, but the frying pan was unacceptable, so off we went into the fire.

"Launch!" cried Rosario.

Responding in unison to this command, we gingerly began moving the boat over the poles toward the sea. Villa and Wilkes ran the poles from the rear to the front as we all leaned into the task. While they repositioned the poles, we caught our breath and then resumed the haul.

As we passed the midway powder kegs, we heard Dad's red alert: "*Jee*-zus! Move, move, go-go-go!"

We responded without looking. Dad's orders left little to the imagination.

Zoe caught a glimpse and screamed, "Raptors! Go-go-go! It's those same ones from the other day!"

There were four of the fifteen-foot monsters about a quarter-mile down the beach and closing fast. We were still thirty feet from the water, but with no time to lay the last of the poles, we had to push the boat through the sand. Fortunately, our adrenaline compensated for the drag. When we made it to the water, Rosario and Joaquin grabbed their muskets and let go at the last stack of powder kegs.

The timing was perfect. Just as the lead monster came upon the powder stash, it blew with a horrific *boom* and black plume. When the smoke cleared, we could see that one of the monsters was down. The others, though dazed, were still on track. Caught with the monsters between them and the fort, Rosario and Joaquin had no choice but to come with us.

"Nothing left to shoot at, Captain," Joaquin shouted, tossing his gun and running for the boat.

Rosario was right behind him as the beasts closed in for the kill. He clamored aboard just as the crew's quick coordinated strokes put us out of reach. The outrigger slipped through the water as if it were alive.

Looking back, I was relieved to see the reptiles give up the chase at the water's edge. In no time, we were out past the breakers. At the top of each rolling swell, we could see the frustrated hunting party back on the beach, venting their rage and scrapping with each other.

"Whatever they are," Dad said, "I guess they can't swim."

"Raptors!" Zoe shouted over the surf as we paddled in unison. "I think they're raptors! I remember seeing them in a movie!"

Rosario snapped back, "Raptors, says you…Satan's retrievers, says I!"

We never took anything Rosario said lightly. The good captain had been right that there's always a hitch.

Joaquin was in the number six seat behind Knox, who had to operate the sail when the time came. As he looked back at Rosario, Joaquin was grim. They hadn't planned on this cruel turn of events. Suddenly, here they were, cut off from Casa Rosario, probably never to return. Their only consolation was that we were still all together.

In the midst of their disappointment and sorrow, there was a spark of potential in Joaquin's words: "We can't change a twist of fate, nor should we want to."

Realizing that he would not be home for supper tonight, Rosario sat staring back for a last look at that spot he had called home for the last hundred years.

Five minutes of quick strokes put us a mile downrange and into the wind, which was a steady fifteen-to-twenty-knot breeze, just waiting for the captain to give the word. While we rowed, he sat still and reflective in the seat in front of Dad, but as we came into the wind he came alive.

Perhaps it was the sea spray that revived Rosario's dormant instincts and filled his lungs with the familiar enthusiasm for life at sea as he gave the order, "Make sail!"

The captain's command infused everyone with a thrill for this new adventure. "Aye, Captain!" was the spirited response as Knox let unfurl the V-shaped sail.

The trade winds were waiting for us to hook up. The aqua swells rising and rolling under a cloudless blue sky reminded me of our Hawaiian adventures. Now that we were finally away from that jungle clamor, this was the most pleasant moment we had had in a long while. As the outrigger took the wind, it cut through the water and, as the wind filled its sail, we were filled with hope and anticipation.

Now, if we could only get lucky...or rather, STAY lucky.

We had decided before we left that Dad would take first watch on the tiller, since he had more than a little experience on outriggers from our days in Hawaii. That made me think of Miko, as soon as we started paddling. Besides teaching surfing, our Tahitian *bradda* had also taught us how to sail an outrigger. With eleven others in an outrigger with no sail, he had made the trip from Tahiti to Hawaii. As a certified Beach Boy, he could make a hat out of palms, play the ukulele, climb a breadfruit tree, make coconut hash, and, of course, surf. He also possessed a captain's license for outriggers. I couldn't help wondering if we would ever see him again.

Our launch point was now almost out of sight. We could barely make out the lagoon and the *Tortuga Diablo.* Rosario and his men gave a last look as the old familiar sight went out of view. Golden sunlight and a flawless azure sky gave this early afternoon a heavenly radiance. Since scudding along with the accommodating wind made rowing unnecessary, we luxuriated in the inactivity, with our paddles resting across our laps.

Keeping a steady course, we had little to do but sit in position and take in the sights. Ahead to our left, the beach gave way to cliffs. To our right was that pipeline that extended across the horizon. From here, it looked twenty-five to thirty feet high. Above it was that eerie, ever-present storm, with its murky green curtain and shimmering lightning streaks.

It wasn't long before the first pangs of restricted movement began to emerge along with a keen tendency for denial. We sailed on over the rise and fall of the rolling swells that were pounding the beach as fifteen-foot breakers. There was stuff on the beach alright, but we were too far out to determine what the irregular shapes were. There were other things, too, only they were moving. We counted two groups of raptor types, about a mile apart from each other.

"Good thing they don't swim," Dad said to Rosario as we all watched the Jurassic beachcombers.

"We haven't seen the last of them, to be sure," said the captain. This was his way of reminding us that, sooner or later, we would be back on the beach.

As the hours slipped by, we could no longer deny our discomforts. The swells were so regular that they were almost hypnotic. In precise intervals, we would rise gently about ten feet and then dip below the horizon. Each swell afforded us our best view of the beach.

A little further on, the beach gave way to sheer cliffs, standing thirty feet above the surf. They were covered with large black blobs, which at first we thought were rocks. However, as the boat rose, they seemed to change shape, and then, as we focused on them, we could see definite movement.

"Giant seals!" I yelled.

The cliffs were covered with them.

"Bigger than the raptors that chased us into the sea!" Zoe cried. "Twenty-five footers..., maybe bigger."

Like the seals we knew at home, these were sunning themselves on the cliffs. As we continued down the coastline, we watched their heads moving back and forth. From time to time, one would push off, diving into the sea below.

We had counted eight divers when the boat suddenly heaved and pitched sideways. It was the kind of unscheduled motion that ignites terror in seafaring men. Even before a reaction begins to take form, there is a queasy realization as information overloads the nervous system. I turned around to look at Zoe, whose face was ashen.

"Now what?" he asked.

Rosario cut him off. "Silence!" he hissed. "It's a leviathan..., and it's beneath us right now!"

He had spoken the truth. *Leviathan* was the only appropriate name for what was passing less than ten feet under us. As the boat continued moving sideways in a most unnatural and unsettling way, our view through the crystalline aquamarine revealed a life form of stupendous breadth swimming swiftly below us.

Our silence lasted a lot longer than it took the monster to pass.

"Maybe it's a sub," Zoe said.

He wasn't being flippant. From what I could see, that was as good a guess as any.

"That thing," said Dad, wide-eyed, "was over a hundred feet, at least! What was it..., some kind of whale?"

No one spoke. Instead, everyone was looking toward the cliff in the direction the thing was moving.

"Thar she blows!" cried Knox.

Right before our eyes, the seals were flying out of the water like missiles and leaping back to the safety of the cliffs. One of them shot out into the air, followed by the leviathan. A wall of water fell away to reveal what looked like a cross between Moby Dick and a giant alligator. Its open mouth completely engulfed the black cliff dweller in midair like a large mouth bass snatching a mosquito. As it fell back into the water with its prey, the ensuing wake countermanded the swells in their perpetual march to the shore. After the brief spastic turbulence, the sea resumed its usual folds, concealing its terrible secrets once again. The short time of silent consideration that followed made it plain we had sailed out into an environment that was every bit as menacing as the jungle we had fled.

Rosario snapped us back into action: "Man your paddles! We'll row while it eats."

As number one, I set a quick pace, and away we went. Ten minutes later, we shipped oars and let the wind take us. The sandy shore was beginning to replace the cliffs once again.

After what we had just seen, we agreed to put in as soon as we could. The horrific events of the last hour had distracted us from the fact that the sun was already sinking out of sight, leaving its crimson bands to replace the day's sapphire with the sable mantle of night. Only half an hour of twilight remained in this terrifying day.

Suddenly, Dad called out, "There's something on the beach!"

"That's something, alright," Zoe said, pointing to it.

"Looks like a Coast Guard cutter, maybe," Dad said excitedly. "It's got a big gun."

Knox wanted to know what it was, too. "Is that one of them things from the future you 'oped to find lyin' 'bout?" he asked.

Dad nodded. As far as he was concerned, this sighting validated his Bermuda Triangle theory. Pointing toward the shore, he said to Rosario, "There's a good chance we'll find things we can use there."

"Well," said the captain, "that's why you came. Secure the sail, Mr. Knox. We'll drift here tonight and go ashore in the morning. Till then, we best keep quiet so as not to attract any trouble."

"Aye, Captain," we all responded.

"It's gonna be a long night," was all Zoe said as we passed out our dinner of water, snake jerky, and apples.

The others hadn't said much since we had gotten under way. The nocturnal beam, which shot out of the mountain as usual, was the only demarcation of land as the last light left the sky.

There was no moon.

This black night had just begun, and already it seemed endless. All we could do was sit in position and watch the shooting stars. Even the awesome cosmic light show lost its appeal in these cramped conditions. One at a time, we would lower our bodies into the tepid water and stretch out. As relative comfort seeped back into our limbs, an overwhelming fear of the deep would force us back into the boat. Nodding in and out of sleep was making this night interminable.

I tried to think of something, *anything*, that would take my attention off our situation.

Shouldn't be hard.... Let's see..., two weeks ago, we were "living our dreams," as Dad would say. Suddenly, our dreams became this inescapable nightmare, where survival is a daily struggle with creatures intent on eating us....

But no matter how I tried to guide myself to memories and thoughts of better days, I couldn't complete a single thought that didn't bring me back to here and now.

The boat was acting funny again—that same cross-wake sensation. Then there was a thud on the hull. Something was checking us out. We all became alert, but as quiet as the dead. The boat was rising, but not from a swell. It was the leviathan, momentarily lifting us out of the water. Then we settled back into the rhythm of the swells. No one made a peep.

After a while, we heard violent splashing somewhere near us. The severe sounds of large bodies slapping the surface kept us paralyzed, certain that we would not survive the night.

Everyone was stiff and sore from sitting still for so long, but the foreboding presence of the colossus beneath us stifled the groans that such discomfort usually elicits from men. As the night wore on, terror transcended fear, which ultimately descended into hopelessness.

Once again, the massive predator passed beneath us, slapping the hull with its fin tip. The blow was not so violent this time, but more like a tap. Then nothing.

"It thinks we're a piece of driftwood," Zoe whispered.

We all wanted to believe him.

Hours dragged on in silence as we tried our best to pass as driftwood. What a night!

At last, the first light brightened the horizon, revealing the dark coastline and the silhouette of the mountain. Themi had called it the Wizard's Hat. I wish we had asked him about the Wizard's laser beam. As we watched it fade from view with the morning light, our attention shifted back to the coastline.

It was evident that we had drifted considerably during the night, because we couldn't see the wrecked cutter anywhere, and the cliffs were out of sight as well.

"Look there!" cried Villa, pointing at the beach. "What's *that?*"

Knox was equally excited: "Another thing from the future, no doubt."

"It's a plane," said Zoe.

He was right. The tail section was protruding unnaturally like a waving hand, beckoning to us. We had had enough of the outrigger, and this sighting was a good piece of luck. If nothing else, it would be an incentive waiting for us on the other side of the fifteen-foot breakers we were about to engage.

Knox snapped the crew into action: "All 'ands, 'eave to! Strike the mainsail!"

As the sail collapsed, and Knox folded it away, he pointed to the approaching breaker. "There's our ride to the beach," he cried, "if we can catch it! Start paddlin' smartly!"

We were all lined up and moving fast enough for the swell Knox had chosen. In Waikiki, this was the fun part of the ride.

Knox called out, "Ship oars!"

Half out of the curl of the pipeline, the boat was flying. The beach was coming up fast as we fell out of the wave and dropped like a rock. It felt as if the boat broke in half as we slammed the shallow white water, but we were still in business. The rest was easy, riding boogie board style right up onto the sand.

Our spirits were now as buoyant as our outrigger. Setting foot back on land felt a lot better than what we had just been through. We secured the outrigger and got on with checking out the crash site. As we started for the plane, our upbeat mood plummeted. There before us were multiple footprints—not human, but lizard-like and huge.

"Not surprising, I guess," Dad said. "At least they're not here now. If these tracks belong to the ones we saw yesterday, they'll be quite a ways from here by now."

We hoped he was right.

The plane was enormous. It had come in on its nose, so the

cockpit was buried in sand. Whoever was in there had been entombed instantly upon arrival.

The port wing was lying twenty-five feet behind the fuselage, which appeared to be intact. We all knew we were looking at our new home for the night.

"No evidence of fire...that's good," Dad said. "It's a Martin Mariner, a rescue plane. I recognize it from my Navy days."

The buccaneers struggled to understand that this mutilated steel hulk had fallen from the sky. Where we saw a downed airplane, Rosario and his men saw a ship that once flew. As they took it in, Dad explained how the wings caught the wind and lifted the plane into the air. They listened, but I don't think they fathomed a word he said.

We found the first two skeletons between the broken wing and the main section. They were sun-bleached, and parts were missing. Soon we came upon six more partial skeletons.

"I'd say they've been here a long time," Dad said, "probably decades."

Staring down at the bones, Zoe said, "My guess is, the raptors got 'em."

As we entered the plane through the rear hatch, we immediately saw that the fuselage contained a number of sealed crates. Two life rafts were equipped with first aid and ration kits. Inside the crates, there were two cases of K-rations, six Thompson machine guns, two cases of grenades, four cases of ammunition, twenty gallons of water still sealed tight in four 5-gallon tins, some folding shovels, and fifty feet of hemp rope.

Zoe, looking like it was Christmas, immediately opened one of the cases of grenades and, holding two up in the air, said, "Man, now we're talking!"

Dad was delighted with the find. "This is strange cargo for a rescue plane," he said, "but I'm not complaining. Alright, let's get organized. First thing is, we bury those poor devils and clean house. This place is gonna feel a lot safer than the outrigger tonight."

The man with the plan was doing his thing.

"Okay, Dad!" Zoe said, grabbing one of the folding shovels and stepping outside.

"You men, go help him with the burying!" Rosario commanded.

The four of them took shovels and followed Zoe out.

I stayed with Dad and Rosario as they continued to inspect the cargo.

"Now, here's something that can give us an edge!" Dad said, after prying open the next crate.

"By the powers, what is it?" Rosario asked.

Holding up a manual, Dad replied, "This is an eighty-one millimeter mortar, Captain. It says here it'll toss a shell a half mile."

"A long reach."

Rosario was becoming a man of few words as each new discovery taxed his comprehension. Dad noticed his mood, but it didn't slow down his show-and-tell tour of the flying ship and its contents.

"We'll see how well it shoots later," he said. "Let's see what else is here."

The plane had two large broken bubble windows about midway on the fuselage.

"It was used for sea rescue," Dad said.

Rosario looked bewildered.

Dad kept talking as he pried open the last case: "From the looks of this gear, this must have been a supply run.... Beautiful!"

"What have ya got?" Zoe asked, returning with the rest of the burial detail. When he looked into the crate, he exclaimed, "Oh, *man!*"

Zoe was having a helluva day as he held an M79 grenade launcher up for all to see. "Now," he said, "we're gonna get some respect around here!"

By the time Dad finished showing us our new armory, we were all pretty hungry.

"Let's give these fifty-year-old K-rations a shot," he said.

"Anything's better than another meal of that bird meat," Zoe said.

I looked at him, surprised at his lack of sarcasm. "I thought you called it snake jerky," I said.

Shaking his head, Zoe replied, "No, it tastes too much like snake to keep joking about it. Anyway, this stuff'll be a welcome change, so let's not mention the other again."

Dad opened a can of the ancient dog food called beef stew. It was alright. Rosario and his men ate it, but not with the enthusiasm that the MREs had produced.

"This isn't bad for a start," Dad said. "I'll bet there's lots more equipment strewn on these beaches. No doubt, we'll find everything we need before much longer."

Eight hours before, we had been all but defenseless. Now we were on a roll, with food and substantial firepower. In addition to the 81mm mortar, there was a smaller 60mm mortar and two M79 grenade launchers, along with two cases of mortar rounds, the grenades, and those lovely Thompsons.

In half an hour, with a quick but meticulous cleaning, Zoe removed all of the packing grease from one of the machine guns. Attaching a clip, he pulled back the bolt and sprayed the sand twenty-five feet in front of where he stood.

Tat-tat-tat-tat-tat.

The short blast was enough to show what these guns could do. Rosario and his men stood open-jawed, watching the sand jump into the air in a straight line.

"I'm not wasting ammo," Zoe said, beaming. "I'm just demonstrating what we have here. This is what I call an upgrade!"

After lunch, Zoe became our gunnery sergeant. It took us two hours to clean out the packing grease, after which we spent the rest of the day learning about the various weapons—first the Thompsons, then the M79s, and finally the mortars. Zoe gave an inclusive demonstration, stressing the need to conserve the ammo.

An enthusiastic war game player, Zoe never intended to pursue a military career, although his level of achievement in computer games gave him a vast technical knowledge of a wide array of weapons. As an avid military buff, he had acquired a fountain of expertise on firepower and tactics.

It was as if Zoe had a special gene. Six years ago, he was a paintball World Cup champion and the youngest member of the infamous Ironmen. All through high school and one year of college, he excelled in triathlons. It was when we became treasure hunters that afternoon between Molokini and Kahoolawe that he was diverted from his usual routine of endurance contests.

As the sun started to slant, we made the fuselage ready for the night. Removing all of the crates, we cleared the space for our shelter. This part of the beach seemed to be free of pests—for now. The sultry breezes and metered rumbling of the surf under the majestic blue blanket created an illusion of the paradise that this abhorrent place could never be.

After supper, we made a fire out of the empty crates and some driftwood. Everyone sat around in silence, lost in his own thoughts under the countless shooting stars of the night sky in this primeval paradox. There would be time in the morning to plan our next few days of survival. Tonight we were ready for sleep. One by one, we slipped through the rear door, quickly finding our spots in the ample space of the Martin Mariner.

Zoe spoke for everyone when he said, "Feels *great* to stretch out!"

After the previous night's ordeal, the fuselage of this old wreck felt like the grand suite at the Hale Pau Hana in Maui. With our new arsenal and supplies, we were enjoying a reinforced sense of security and confidence about our decision to venture out from Casa Rosario. We had survived another day full of the stuff that made our lives a deadly adventure, a game that could not last.

As we all settled down for the night, Knox said, "Things are lookin' up, lads."

We didn't expect any callers, so, with the hatch secured, we felt no need to post a watch, and all fell fast asleep as soon as our heads touched the deck.

"Eli!"

Zoe was shaking me awake into an atmosphere of darkness and terror just as I was in the middle of a vivid nightmare about that raptor of two days before. We were locked in, eye-to-eye again.

"They're back!" he said.

Zoe's words were stinging the funny bone of my mind as I began to comprehend. Even though no one was stirring, I assumed that everyone else was awake.

As Zoe grabbed his Thompson, the incessant hissing outside sounded like buckets of water being thrown on molten steel. The whole fuselage lurched, and then rocked back and forth.

"How many?" I asked, feeling around for my own gun.

"More than one," Dad answered. "Zoe, you do the shooting

if it comes to it."

"Arm yourselves with those new weapons, men," Rosario called, "and wait for the word."

The sound of ammo clips being fastened to the Thompsons told me that Zoe had taught the men well.

As Zoe slipped a fresh clip into place and pulled back the bolt, we could barely make out a dark shape passing the broken window across from us.

"Can't see anything," Zoe said softly. "How long till it gets light?"

"Shouldn't be too long," Dad whispered. "We've got to wait till we can see well before we make our move."

"Hope *they* don't mind waiting," Zoe said. He wasn't joking.

The tails of the beasts slammed the plane from time to time, as if they were trying to scare us out. Rosario and his men crouched by the hatch like a boarding party, fully armed, ready, and waiting for action.

"They know we're in here," Dad whispered. "They've done this before. That's what all those partial skeletons were about... They can smell us. That means there will be more and more voracious raptors out there before long."

That was all Zoe had to hear. Slipping out his flashlight and shining it on the case of M79 ammo, using Themi's bowl to cover the escaping light, he said, "We're gonna need these. Let's get ready!"

When we didn't respond, he spun around to see why not.

We were transfixed by what was happening with Themi's bowl. As the red beam of light shot out of the top, I realized it was the Wizard's Hat, a replica of the mountain. Its symbols came to life, animated by the light from within. We almost forgot the problem at hand as we noticed new things on the bowl that weren't visible without the inner light.

But our focus was suddenly interrupted by a raptor landing on the roof. The horrendous thud did not tear open our steel compartment, but inverted the fuselage considerably.

"*Jee*-zus!"

Dad was staring at a reptilian head poking in through one of the broken bubble windows, a shrill hiss emanating from its drooling, gaping jaws.

"Everybody down!" Zoe shouted, blazing a quick double burst.

Tat-tat-tat, tat-tat-tat.

The beast recoiled from the rain of stinging bullets with a ghastly shriek. Then its black featureless head reappeared in the window, to which Zoe responded with a second burst from his Thompson. This time the beast staggered out of sight, screeching as it shook its head.

Our fear had become a vicious, jagged sensation of hopelessness that threatened to snap our spines as we heard the hungry reptiles hissing in the night.

"Those babies are *big*," said Zoe, "but I know we must be hurting them with head shots like that." Then, looking at the navigator's window, a little bubble hatch on the top of the fuselage, he added, "When we can see something, we can surprise them from there with the M79."

The trouble was that we were in a tin can, and these guys were going to play kick the can until they won. The nocturnal prowlers were thrashing around spastically, making a terrible racket. Then came an eerie five minutes of silence.

Suddenly, they hit us all at once. The roof started to cave in and crumble. Again, one of them poked its head into the window. Zoe was waiting and let him have it. This time we could see its features. That was good news and bad news.

The good news was that it was morning, and we could see our targets. The bad news was that it was terrifying to see the raptor up close, eye to eye, knowing that it wanted to eat us.

"Take over here," Zoe told Joaquin, moving to the bubble top. "Dad, feed me rounds when I get set up."

Eager to get into the fight, the captain, Knox, Villa, and Wilkes took up their guns and pulled back the bolts, reacting with the speed and precision of seasoned troops. As they aimed their Thompsons with anticipation, Dad pulled the grenades over to Zoe.

"Create a diversion," Zoe called down to us. "I need time to squeeze through the donut hole."

Dad looked at me: "Grenades! Two! Window!"

"You got it!"

The next minute, with pin in hand, I was ready for the word. Outside it sounded like more beasts were arriving. Their incessant clamor was getting louder as the sun came up on the horizon.

Zoe finally had the light he needed.

"Ready!" he shouted, opening the hatch and throwing it back as I tossed the first grenade as far as I could, and then the second.

Boom!

Not that far, I thought.

Boom!

With the second explosion, Zoe was up and firing.

Ahrk! Poom! Clang! Boom!

Zoe's first shot with the RPG blew a gaping hole in the breast of his target.

"There's a lotta them!" he shouted as Dad passed him another round. "Get on those weapons! Let 'em have it!"

Rosario threw the side door open, and Knox jumped out with his Thompson blazing. Villa followed and knelt beside Knox, his rocket launcher at the ready. As one raptor staggered off and then toppled over, another round exploded in their midst. Villa selected a raptor that was unscathed and fired his M79 at it. What a shot! As Villa let loose, the beast turned and opened its mouth in protest, only to swallow the projectile. The reptile seemed to know that it had screwed up. A distinct look of regret came over its face as its head exploded.

The Dali-esque image of the headless raptor staggering about had me swimming in waves of horror and adrenaline. The raptors came unglued, shrieking when they saw their crony running around like that. After one-and-a-half laps around the front yard, the headless form collapsed. That's when the others cleared out...all except the two dead ones.

We had won our first battle with the raptors. These guys were becoming a daily hassle. Our tin can shelter was looking pretty shabby, and now we had a couple of tons of dinosaur bait in our front yard. Problems were still stacking up faster than solutions.

By the time Rosario and his men finished reloading their new weapons and came over to us, we had already inflated the two life rafts and were busy loading the mortars and ammo into them. The buccaneers glared at us, obviously puzzled.

"If you are preparing for another attack," said the captain, "it will be our last stand, to be sure."

Dad stood up from the ammo case he was moving and matched Rosario's glare.

"One thing's for sure, Captain..., we can't stay here another hour." Pointing skyward, he said, "Everything's at least fifteen feet tall in this place." He was referring to the pterodactyls that were gathering high above us—huge, powerful reptiles with the advantage of flight. "This place is gonna get real busy, real soon. We have to make a move." Dad was ahead of the curve and already carrying out his plan. "Okay, here's what I've got. We'll fill these rafts with everything we can take and still float."

None of the pirates liked that idea, especially Rosario, who cut in, "You don't mean to go back out to sea?"

Dad grimaced. "Of course not. I mean, all we have now for survival are these weapons and food supplies, and the fastest way for us to get away from this spot is to run down the beach pulling the rafts over the edge of the water."

Their negative attitude changed as they pictured Dad's plan, realizing that it would be our best move. If we could last, maybe we could find the means to escape this place.

After moving down the beach at a good clip, we took our first break. Looking back, we could see the hideous flying lizards still circling overhead, marking the distant point from which we had started. The beach extended for miles, and then there would be more cliffs to deal with. As we continued toward them, I thought about those herds of raptors we had seen from the outrigger, moving down the beach. Scampering over the water's edge, looking every which way, afraid of being exposed, we were not unlike any other smaller life form on this island. Never for a moment were we safe from sudden attack by the wide variety of creatures that craved our flesh.

As the pounding surf relentlessly hammered the beach beneath the sweltering sun, we pressed on along the foam. By now, it was late afternoon, and we were desperate to find shelter, any place that would stave off the multitude of creatures that would get their chance at us sooner or later.

"'Ello!" Knox called, stopping and pointing. "A ship, there in the shadow of the cliffs.... And beached, by god!"

He was right. The dark silhouette was distinct. Even from this distance, we could tell it was a large ship.

"Never a dull moment," Dad said.

As we closed the distance, we could see that it was some

kind of tanker. The towering hull was almost fully exposed, with its bow dug into the beach and the breakers exploding over the stern. The name was faded but legible: *Hornet Queen.*

Once again, Rosario and his men came face to face with the future, marveling at her appearance. This was a supertanker made of steel with no masts. Explaining these things was easy for Dad, compared to trying to explain petroleum and its purposes in the world we knew.

Standing next to the massive hull out of water felt surreal. The *Hornet Queen* looked like a great steel fortress with no access except by an amidships exterior staircase that extended halfway down the side. There was no telling how long the great ship had been here like this. With no signs of life, we could only imagine how many skeletons we would find if and when we could get aboard.

"No trace of an oil spill," Dad said. "I wonder if it's still full." He was thinking out loud, hoping for some answers. "If we could get up to that stairway, we'd be in business."

Suddenly, there were priorities that superseded our latest discovery.

"Uh-oh!" Zoe cried, running toward the rafts. "We've got company! Get the big guns...*quick!*"

When we looked down the beach, we could see them still at least half a mile away, bobbing up and down, and closing fast. An all too familiar wave of terror electrified the company as we scrambled to repel another attack from our nemeses.

As Dad and Zoe aimed the heavy mortar, I had the first shell ready to go.

Dad moved on to the small mortar, shouting to Rosario, "Arm your men, Captain!" not seeing that this was already done.

After a final adjustment, Zoe hollered, "Ready! Load!"

As soon as I dropped the projectile down the pipe, it fired. This first round hurled over the herd, exploding unnoticed behind them. So far they weren't getting our message and continued to close on us.

Another quick adjustment and we fired again. This shell was more effective, exploding on the beach in front of the charging dinosaurs. Taken by surprise, they turned and started to run back.

Zoe let another one go. The overall effect was to temporarily suspend the creatures' forward progress, giving us enough time to set up a symbolic barricade of ammo crates between the flesh-eaters and us.

"Even if we do make a stand here," Rosario said, "we won't last." Then, pointing to the weather deck of the tanker, he added, "We've got to get up there."

He was right. Only the high ground could save us now.

"Here they come again!" Zoe called. "Drop fifteen!" He adjusted the heavy mortar fifteen degrees downward. "Load!"

I dropped another shell into the pipe.

Chank-POOM!

"On target!" I shouted.

Zoe's first shot hit one of the lead beasts, which blew apart in front of the startled herd.

Chank-POOM!

The second salvo blew up in their midst. Once again, they turned tail and ran.

Now it was Dad who was urging us on to the steel sanctuary.

"Somehow," he said, "I don't think they're gonna give up so easily. We need to get aboard that tanker! Captain, if you and your men can find a way to reach that ladder, we could hoist everyone and everything to safety."

The only access to the towering weather deck was dangling halfway down the ship's thirty-foot-high hull off the port side. Rosario led his men into the water toward the stairway that dangled fifteen feet above the surf. After a moment, they decided to form a human ladder to get a man to the first step. Prevailing through the impetuous surf was the first phase of this life-or-death challenge.

With Knox and Villa in position at the bottom, Wilkes climbed onto their shoulders, followed by Joaquin, who stood on him. But their first attempt failed. As Joaquin made a desperate grab at the stairway to the future, he and Wilkes toppled into the water.

After the men quickly reassembled the human pyramid, Joaquin was just climbing into position when Rosario shouted, "Here they come again!"

His warning snapped Dad, Zoe, and me into action before we could see if the acrobats had accomplished their goal.

The raptors were stampeding straight toward us. As they

reached the point of the last barrage, Zoe and I once again fired the large mortar in rapid succession.

"Still out of range for me," Dad said, eager to join in the barrage.

"That's a good thing, Dad," Zoe said. "Maybe we can *keep* them out of range."

But that was too much to hope for. The furious beasts were coming alright, and moments later Dad's complaint was irrelevant, for we could hear their hisses as they closed in.

In the midst of all the commotion before us, the sound of hope came hollering over the surf: "Let's go, mates, we're in!"

Looking up at the boarding party, we saw Joaquin waving to us from the ship's ladder.

Rosario called, "Throw down some rope!"

"We need to get everything aboard," Dad called. "Zoe and Eli, you keep us covered, and the rest of us will move the supplies."

He handed his mortar shell to me, grabbed two ammo crates, and started toward the ship.

"Okay, Dad," I said.

Zoe let another round fly, and then another, stalling the advance once again.

As Dad, Knox, and Villa stood in the water, tying supplies to the rope, Rosario, Joaquin, and Wilkes hoisted them up to the weather deck. When everything was safely aboard, Knox and Villa shimmied up the rope, and Dad came back to get us.

"Okay, boys," Dad said, "let's grab this stuff and board the

As usual, he pointed out the positive side of our hopeless predicament.

"By the powers!" called Rosario. "A castle on a ship!"

He and his men were awestruck by the massive proportions of the vessel that was to be our new refuge—a ship larger than anything they could have imagined.

"Let's check it out before it gets dark!" Dad said, starting toward the four-story superstructure.

"Wonder what happened to her crew," I said.

My remark turned Zoe's head. "Maybe we'll find out as we look around," he said. "A skeleton here, a mummy there..., *you know.*"

As usual, his sarcasm made us cringe with its tinge of probability.

"First thing we'll do," he said, hoping to find some creature comforts, "is check out the crew's quarters." As we crossed the football field–sized weather deck, he added, "At least we've found a place where we can be safe for a while."

The last light of the day had succumbed to the evening sky. We had missed another sunset during our preoccupation with the raptors.

"This ship hasn't been here very long, from the looks of her," Dad said, trying to see through the darkness. "We'll be better off outside on the deck tonight. Tomorrow we'll see what we have here."

Everyone concurred. We made camp outside, next to a door on the port side, just in case we had to run in for cover. It was a hot night. After sharing the ration kits high above the surf and sand, we felt reasonably safe and thankful to have found this waylaid tanker. It felt like a fortress, whose security allowed us to doze under a celestial resplendence with the sounds of breakers splashing on the fantail.

Everyone was already up and moving about the ship when I awoke.

"Good morning, son," Dad said to me with a smile. "Guess what we found?"

"Don't tell me...a friendly dinosaur? And he can take us all back home?"

Choosing to ignore my attempt at humor, Dad came out with it: "On the stern, there's a fully equipped survival launch..., all set to go!"

I sprang to my feet. Rosario and his men were on the fantail, looking over every inch of the survival craft as if it were some kind of strange-looking longboat. With short decks fore and aft, the craft was equipped with a telescopic hood that could retract from both ends to the middle, leaving only the center section enclosed. When battened down, it looked unsinkable.

As I arrived, Zoe was just climbing out of the launch, clearly feeling upbeat. "Looks good to me," he said. "Just what we were hoping for."

Dad said to Rosario, "This boat could get us out of here."

"Get us out of here, says you! How in hell can we catch the wind without sails?"

"We don't need wind," said Dad. "You see that? It's called a propeller. It will move the boat faster than the wind."

With a glazed look, Rosario muttered, "Says you!"

"It's another device from the future, Captain," Dad said. "You'll just have to take it on faith."

Rosario shook his head and said no more.

"Dad," I said, "what do you make of that empty boat rack?"

Dad thought for a moment. "That's probably why there's no bones about," he said at last. "The crew must have abandoned ship before she beached here."

"It's anybody's guess," Zoe said, "*why* they abandoned ship."

This discovery was a great way to wake up, but now we had to deal with something more pressing. The raptors were back, devouring their two dead companions, which were lying on the beach, one within fifty yards of us, and the other within twenty. Each carcass was a buffet as the beasts fought over every morsel. Fortunately, the constant pounding of the breakers muffled the racket. We stayed away from the side rail, hoping they would forget about us.

Villa said softly, "The wind...she is in our favor. Maybe they won't notice us. We best stay out of their sight until they clear out."

Villa usually didn't say very much, but when he did, it was to the point.

"It's time," Dad said, "to search the ship and see what we can find. Stay out of sight and be as quiet as possible." He had that familiar gleam in his eye as he ignited our common lust for treasure.

It was with spirited anticipation that we started our search. With the acquisition of the fully equipped launch, we had already reached our objective. We would be leaving soon, but not before finding what else there was that might help us.

The first deck was taken up with the pumping controls and utility lockers. On the second deck, there were the crew's quarters and also a well-stocked sickbay and galley. After a while, our search turned up the usual things—flares, first-aid supplies, and life jackets. There was a complete machine shop with fuel and tools. The food lockers were full of spoiled food, but there were also canned goods, including peaches and pears, veggies, and more beef stew. In the crew's quarters, there were real beds.

The highlight of the search was a pair of gas generators. We were elated when we discovered them. Not only would we have some lights tonight, but they were the key to our freedom. We would be able to charge the batteries on the launch. Acquiring the generators was like finding two treasure chests.

Rosario and his men didn't understand why we were so excited, but they were happy for us.

There were two lookout posts, port and starboard. The former served as a safe vantage point from which to observe the feeding frenzy on the beach. The coastline stretched as far as the eye could see on the port side. The starboard side revealed cliffs in the distance, before the coastline curved out of sight.

It was almost noon by the time the herd of predators moseyed back down the beach, leaving no trace of the ones that fell.

The crew had spread out all over the superstructure in search of useful stores. Later, when we reassembled to compare our findings, Zoe was animated as he came in from the lookout. "Guess what?" he said. "There are solar panels all across the top of the superstructure. That means there might be some electricity available."

As Rosario's quizzical expression indicated, we were speaking "future talk" again, which was happening at almost every juncture now.

Dad turned to the pirates, trying to explain. "The same power," he said, "that lights the flashlight might be here on this ship." He left it at that because they had a glassy look, struggling to comprehend what he was saying. "Zoe," he added, "see if you can trace the wires from the solar panels and figure where we can plug in, while the rest of us check out the pumping room to see if there's any oil aboard."

After checking out the gauges for the tanks in the pumping room, Dad said to Rosario and me, "From what I can tell, these oil tanks are empty. If we could find a sounding tool, we could make sure, but the amount of oil on board isn't important. We'd better stay focused on our objective."

Escaping from here was Dad's priority, so the question of how much, if any, oil remained in the holds was dropped for the moment as we returned to the waiting lifeboat. We had a portable charger plugged into the generator, and its jumper cables connected to the little ship of hope. At first, the generator was hard to start. The launch's engine had a similar reluctance before submitting to Dad coaxing. After it ran for ten minutes, we pronounced it ready, and shut it off to conserve fuel. Now that there was little left for us to do, the time when we would be on our way out of here was imminent.

All this while, poor Rosario, exposed to an unending series of modern technologies and terms, was suffering from a perpetual state of psycho-blur. This alienation had reduced him to a dependency on us that made him feel impotent.

Dad understood the look these things gave to Rosario's twisted face. Maybe it was wrong to have seduced these poor survivors out of their ageless habitat and into our quest to return to a world they didn't understand. Dad's tone remained upbeat as he tried to share his optimism with the captain. "That little boat," he said, "will cut through the water at twenty knots. It has an engine…a source of power equal to four hundred horses."

At this, the captain's rumpled eyebrow rose. He simply couldn't believe the power of four hundred horses. But he had seen enough of these new gadgets by now to know not to ask too much about them. The answers were always confusing. It was better to try to catch on slowly as things became familiar. He longed to return to his cliffside home, but that was not meant to be. His command was ebbing with each new development. Obsolescence would be his new role in all of this.

Looking at the captain with compassion, Dad said, "We can't

stay here forever.... Let's plan our next move."

Rosario stared back at Dad, but said nothing.

Dad wasn't fazed by the captain's morose silence. "When we complete our search," he said, "we'll eat and make plans."

"Make plans, says you.... Choose your *poison*, says I." And Rosario turned his back on us, staring sullenly out to sea.

"Pessimism is the enemy of creativity," Dad always said. But this time he chose to keep it to himself, giving the captain a few moments alone.

Finally, Rosario turned back to us and asked, "You say this boat can be lowered away on its own, with no help from us?"

"That's right, Captain. You just turn it on with this switch." But to Dad's amazement, when he flicked the dead switch, red, yellow, and green lights suddenly came on.

Rosario jumped back, more startled from Dad's reaction than from the glowing lights.

Next there was music.

"Born in the USA.... I was born in the USA...."

Bruce Springsteen was singing from the ship's speakers!

Knox and the men came running out to see what was happening. Then Zoe appeared on deck.

"There's plenty of power stored," he said. "All I did was turn it on. I traced the solar panel connecting to the transformer room, and there it was!"

"Well done, son!" Dad said, delighted.

The sounds of Bruce Springsteen had a miraculous effect on the buccaneers. The music of the future transformed their growing moodiness into a joyous anticipation of what might be waiting in the promised land. Our morale, too, was at the highest it had been since we started this odyssey. Salvation felt like a distinct possibility.

Zoe sang out with Bruce, and Dad and I joined in.

"Born in the USA...."

Rosario and his men looked on, smiling as they watched us sing. Dad was happy to see this effect on them.

The sun was also at its highest point.

"Let's use the rest of the day to rest up before our next adventure," Dad said. "That will start first thing in the morning."

No one objected.

"Let's eat," said Zoe. "I'm getting mighty hungry!"

Everybody liked that idea. Today's treat was peaches. We found a gallon tin and made short work of it. After lunch, some of us stretched out on the beds and caught up on our sleep. I had long since lost track of what day it was, but this seemed like a Sunday afternoon.

Later, I awoke to a sultry breeze and strands of Cat Stevens, singing "Where Do the Children Play?"

Zoe was standing in front of a mirror, wearing a new pair of Navy jeans and a blue shirt.

"The showers are working now," he said to me. "Better get one while you can."

I was in the shower almost before Zoe finished his sentence. But I had barely rinsed myself when the pressure went limp and then quit.

"I guess Rosario and the boys got carried away," Zoe said when I returned to the crew's quarters, looking perplexed. "They took *very* long showers while you were sleeping. Anyway, there's new clothes down the hall on the left."

I couldn't get there fast enough. Within minutes, I was enjoying my new outfit.

"The pirates," Zoe said, "had mixed feelings about dressing in modern clothes. What really got to them was trading in their hundred-year-old sandals for white canvas deck shoes."

Zoe's matter-of-fact tone, the music, and the renewing shower and clothes were a new variation in this surreal existence, whose overall effect was a vivid reminder of normalcy.

Everyone now had on new blue denim jeans and blue work shirts, just like Navy issue, and we all looked ten pounds lighter with the dirt off.

It was now early evening as we all stood on top of the super-structure, watching the sunset and contemplating the pipeline, tomorrow's threshold of destiny.

Breaking the silence, Rosario snarled, "We're caught up here like rats. There's only one place to go from here, and we'll be there soon enough."

The captain had been quiet for most of the afternoon, but now his brooding bubbled over like hot candle wax.

Knox, who grimaced as he strove to hold on to the moment we were enjoying, found himself defending their situation to Captain Pessimist.

"It's been a struggle everyday, Cap'n, that's true," he said. "But we've been lucky, and we 'ave found and seen wondrous things, to be sure.... We'll get through this, Cap'n."

Rosario simply nodded as the boatswain's words brought a background chorus of agreement from the rest of the crew, who sought to put some wind back in Rosario's sails.

But the captain only glowered at them, lamenting, "I realize now that I was content to be prisoner here and to see how long I could remain thirty-five years old."

Dad let Rosario's words settle before he replied, "We have to put one foot in front of the other until we can see our way clear of this place. I figure we've got three choices." All eyes turned to Dad. "One, we can get the boat started and head straight out. Two, we can climb the mountain in search of the laser. Or three, we can stay here. As for continuing to search for more equipment, that's no longer necessary, since we now have the means to escape."

Rosario responded with conviction, "I have no desire to climb the mountain, and I don't believe a sea escape is possible. I feel that a life-or-death struggle to get back to our fort would be worth the risk."

Dad wasn't buying this plan any more than Rosario was buying Dad's. "When we started out," Dad said, "it was to find the means of escape and then get away. Well, that's exactly what we have accomplished. Tomorrow, we'll get that survival boat cranked up, and with a little more luck, we'll be back on the mainland and away from this nightmare."

There was silence as we let Dad's words sink in. So far, his predictions had worked out. At any rate, the three of us were not wavering from our original plan to escape.

As the sun disappeared behind the mountain, the ship's night lights came on—an unlikely sight in the primeval jungle setting. In contrast with the melee that took place here yesterday, tonight it was calm and quiet except for the pounding surf.

But then, sounding concerned, Zoe said, "The lights may not be a good idea."

Dad nodded. "Right, we don't want to attract the wrong types.... And that's all I've seen around here."

"The switches are below in the transformer room," I said. "I'll go and shut them down."

"Leave the crew's quarters on, Eli," Dad said.

"Roger that."

As I went below to find the appropriate switches on the starboard side, the dazzling red corona of the setting sun was transforming the blue evening sky. A vivid molten red hue came over the savage jungle prison we were trying so desperately to escape. The sound of the waves splashing on the stern was even louder in the transformer room.

Just when I had thrown the switches and was starting back the way I had come, I realized, like a slap in the face, that what I had thought was the sound of the waves was really some reptilia off the forward starboard side. Their unrelenting hissing was increasing to a hideous screeching, making it easy now to discern between surf and snake. Peering over the rail, I was able to make out several of the two-legged lizards congregating in the twilight on the beach near the bow.

I was spooked, but decided to keep my observation to myself, so the crew might get a good night's sleep. I was reasonably sure we were out of the lizards' reach up here. Tomorrow would be soon enough to deal with this latest appearance of the insatiable beasts.

Except for the compartments we were using, the ship was now completely dark, for the moon wasn't up yet. The electric lights gave the superstructure the appearance of a dimly lit lighthouse. It was a beacon, I thought, not for warning ships at sea but for beckoning creatures in the night—like a sign at Joe's All Night Burgers.

When I returned from the transformer room with a long flashlight that I had picked up there, I said, "These batteries still have some juice."

"Hey, that reminds me!" Zoe replied, pulling out the sack from his stash. "Remember what happened the other night in the plane?" He slipped Themi's bowl out and then the disposable flashlight. Placing the bowl over the light, he flicked on the switch. "Check it out!"

Zoe walked toward the darkened part of the room with his back to us, then turned to face us, holding what looked like some kind of orb with points of light projecting moving images faintly on the walls and ceiling. A single red beam shot out from the top into the darkness, illuminating his face.

"There's some kind of story or something on here," he said.

"Bring it here," Dad commanded from the table, "and we'll turn out the lights."

Zoe had everyone's attention except mine as I struggled to keep my horrible secret a little while longer. My heart was in my throat, since I knew that the monsters were still intent on having us.

After passing the light and the bowl around the table, everyone agreed that the layout of the lines and symbols must be clues to the mountain's mystery. Then something quite remarkable happened. As the disposable flashlight began to fade, the bowl no longer projected images to the walls and ceiling. Instead, in the diminished light, a focused map appeared with symbols that seemed to be moving. There was a river encircling the mountain and a man sitting with folded arms in a canoe. At one point in the river, there was a junction with an intersecting waterway. This was marked by a symbol resembling, of all things, a saucer craft. Just above the saucer, there was a symbol composed of three triangles, each within the other, the innermost being the brightest. Upon closer examination, we saw that the top of Themi's model had a red gem in the center.

As we pondered these things, the weak batteries in the flashlight went completely dark.

Rosario and his men, who seemed to be seeing the mountain for the first time, became frustrated when the light quit.

Zoe grabbed my flashlight and put it back under the bowl, but it would no longer show us its message.

"Too much light," Zoe said, taking a sports magazine from a

nearby table and tearing an order form from its center. When he passed the piece of red paper over the lens of the flashlight, the mountain's map reappeared.

"A saucer!" I shouted. "Like the one we found!"

I still had the pictures we had taken of the saucer lying on the ocean floor.

The captain cut in, "According to this map, we could return to our stockade by way of the river." Rosario had clearly had enough. "Out here," he continued, "we are committed to fight for every day we live...and for *what*? I can see here the way back to the only home we'll ever have now." His tone was fateful, reflecting his certainty that the odds were stacked against us—and the other pirates looked equally discouraged.

"Aye," said Knox, "that beastie is still out there, waitin' to swallow us like so many goldfish."

"I didn't want to say anything," said Wilkes, "but I'd be content to stay in the times we know."

"I like you, *hombres*," said Villa, "but I'll be sticking with my mates."

It was becoming clear that a parting of the ways was likely.

"I agree, Captain," Dad said, "that whatever our next move is, it won't be without the usual struggle. But for us, returning to the stockade is not an option. My boys and I are determined to find a way back to our world...or die trying."

For the moment, that was enough said on that subject.

"I need some fresh air," said Knox. "I'll be goin' down to the weather deck."

Anxious to see if he would discover my secret, I followed him down.

Out on deck, the rising moon was lighting up the clear night sky. As soon as we got outside, we heard a commotion coming from off the port bow on the beach. Knox leaned over the rail to get a look.

"Raptors!" he cried.

We could see three thrashing about in the sand, intentionally slapping the hull with their tails.

My secret was out. Rushing back to the crew's quarters, Knox yelled, "They're back! Three raptors, maybe more, on the beach off the port bow!"

"Get the weapons!" Zoe called, grabbing an M-79 as the rest of us pulled back the bolts on our Thompsons.

"Better switch on the ship's spotlights," Dad said to me, "so we can see what's up."

I ran to the bridge to throw the switch.

Thwack! Thwack!

As they pounded the bulkhead with their mighty tails, the *Hornet Queen's* four spotlights came on in quick succession, illuminating the beach like daylight along the fringe of the ship's massive shadow. There were at least a dozen of the wily reptiles visible in the bright light, thrashing the sand and thumping, and occasionally looking up at us, their gaping maws emitting a constant gurgling hiss.

Once again, terror ignited our frazzled nerves as we came to grips with our bleak situation.

"Maybe it's some kind of ritual they do," Dad said, thinking out loud as always when he didn't have answers.

"Well," Zoe said, "they've sure got our attention, if that's what they want."

"Yeah, that's what they want alright!" Dad said, remembering the night the monsters raided the Martin Mariner. "These raptors are ambush artists."

Screech, clang, thud!

Hearing these sounds behind us, we spun around to see one of the beasts coming over the railing to the deck by way of the amidship ladder.

"*Jee*-zus!"

Dad started blazing with his Thompson.

Another raptor head appeared over the railing. Zoe fired at the first intruder as it turned to get its bearings. The explosion spun it around, sending it reeling off toward the bow. When Dad and Rosario poured on the hot lead, the dazed creature toppled over the side. Zoe fired at the second boarder, blowing a gaping hole in its neck. As it took the blast, the raptor grabbed the ladder with both claws, then fell backward to the shallows below, taking the ladder with it.

Now the moon was high in the sky and was coloring the night with blue light. As we all peered over the side, we could see the other raptors moving on the beach below us.

"They never left," Villa said with a grimace. "They won't quit till they have us."

"Without the ladder, I don't think they can climb up here,"

Dad said, trying to console him.

"Just the same," said Zoe, "I'm not sleeping outside tonight. Better keep the lights on, Eli. At least we'll be able to see them if they come again."

"You're right, Zoe," Dad said, "the beasts would never fit into this maze of passageways and compartments. So, let's get a good night's sleep while we can."

"Listen up, everyone!" Zoe commanded. "We're getting low on ammo. We've gotta make it last till we can get outta here, so don't waste any shots tomorrow. Make every one count!"

My brother was a proven asset in times like this.

I was dreaming of the Vineyard Haven ferry docking with a flurry of seagulls clambering loudly overhead when I was rudely jerked into reality.

"On deck!" Zoe ordered, bursting into the compartment.

I was on my feet before I even thought to ask why.

"Big birds," he said. "They're circling and diving off the starboard side."

"Big birds?" Dad said, getting up. "That can't be good news. Let's go to the lookout and see what's happening."

He led the way down the catwalk to the starboard lookout pod.

"*Jee*-zus!" Dad was pointing at the hull. "There's a gaping hole wide enough to fit a car through."

That was no exaggeration. The protruding jagged edges of the huge rupture were a silent statement of the injustice the *Hornet Queen* had once suffered. It was becoming brutally obvious that there were still things about this ship we hadn't discovered. But at the moment we had other problems.

"Look at that!" Dad cried, pointing at two, then three baby raptors, which were scurrying out of the hole and across the beach toward the tree line.

Before anyone could utter a word, the first infant sprinter gave it up to a pterodactyl that was swooping in only a few yards in front of us. The giant vulture snatched its breakfast delicacy and made for the cliffs, its sanctuary from competitors, with the newborn flailing and screeching in its claws.

Our day was heating up in more ways than one. The cloudless, cerulean horizon steaming in a golden haze was all but obscured behind the black iridescent soaring reptilia that were massing in anticipation of a fruitful swoop or two. As the first three hatchlings were captured, three or four more made a break for the jungle cover. But each time, their escape was thwarted by the flying lizards, who swept in one after another. When they noticed us, they dove toward us as if to test our response. The northern sky was black with pterodactyls.

And they kept coming. The flock was so thick that I wondered how many would succeed in winning one of the delectable reptilian tidbits. I saw at least ten newborns scamper for the tree line, but fail. Now hundreds of the flying giants were closing in. Their ambitious plunges indicated that they were flying on empty.

"Everybody back inside!" Dad shouted.

As we ran down the catwalk, the birds were getting bolder.

Dad was the last one in, as Zoe reappeared at the door, pulling back the bolt on his Thompson. A few quick bursts put the pterodactyls on a different vector.

Inside, Dad said, "Looks like we're sitting on a hatch of raptors!"

Rosario had seen his luck running out ever since he was shanghaied by circumstance. Again, with rage and defeat shaping his words, he said, "Hatch, says you.... The gates of Hell, says I. They'll have us soon, or we'll stay prisoners in this iron coffin!"

But Knox wasn't giving up. "We beat 'em yesterday, Cap'n," he said. "And we'll beat 'em again today!"

"Aye, Captain," Villa added. "We'll beat them every day until we get back home."

The rest of the crew nodded in agreement.

"How long can this last?" Zoe asked. "A day, maybe two, before the feeding is over?"

His question was rhetorical—meant to start Dad's planning mechanism.

And Dad did in fact kick in. "Maybe," he said, "if we keep a low profile while they're here, they'll forget us and leave. In the meantime, we have what we need to hole up in here for a while."

Zoe disagreed. "I don't think they'll be forgetting about us, Dad. They almost boarded us last night!"

In fact, no one was buying Dad's latest attempt at positive thinking.

"The ammo's almost gone except for the flares," said Zoe. "We still have plenty of those."

The pterodactyls' gourmet lunch wore on as they plucked the baby raptors from life, one after another. For our part, none of us wanted to just sit and wait for things to happen.

Ben Wilkes voiced his racking impatience with our situation. "No signs of letting up," he said. "I wonder how many of the buggers are left?"

As always, Zoe wanted to take action. "Let's go get a look into that second hold," he said. "Maybe we can get some answers. The hatch can be rolled back from the bridge."

Dad nodded. "Okay, Zoe," he said, "you go to the bridge and open the hatch over the middle hold. Eli and I will go down on deck and take a look. Captain, you and your men can provide us with cover fire if we need it."

Rosario pulled back the bolt on his Thompson. Despite our recent differences about our next destination, for the time being we were still working together as a team. This trait of Rosario's to be so pessimistic, on one hand, and yet a complete team player, on the other, gave me a warm admiration for the man.

There were vents on both sides of each of the three holding tanks. Dad and I burst out of the starboard door and ran down along the rail. The all-day brunch was still the center attraction on the beach, so we arrived unnoticed as Zoe opened the hatchway from the bridge. A paralyzing panic swept through me as we peered down upon the repugnant scene illuminated in the shaft of light.

We could see layers upon layers of seething, slime-covered eggs in various stages of hatching. Some of the hatchlings had already cleared their shells. The newborns sat there looking dazed. With gaping mouths, they emitted feeble squeaks and gurgles, sounding much like human babies. They were a long way from that time when most creatures would give them a wide berth—if indeed they would ever live to see such a day.

Dad flashed his light into the darkness to reveal a mature raptor knee deep in eggs, on which it was gorging. Stepping into the narrow beam of light, the ravenous raptor jerked its head upward, opened its drool-dripping maw, and gave a terrible screech, so out of proportion to its size that it had a nauseating effect upon every fiber of my being.

Dad was aghast. All he could say was, "We've *gotta* get *outta* here!"

When we ran back to the superstructure, everyone was waiting for our report. The expressions on our faces transferred to theirs even before we spoke.

"We're sitting on a can of live bait!" Dad said, breaking the news. "There are *thousands* of eggs in the middle hold, which are hatching as we speak!"

Rosario shot back, "Trapped again! Soon everything for miles around will be arriving for their share of the feast."

His prediction was manifesting as he spoke. Just then a herd of much larger raptors came running out of the jungle and down the beach toward the ship, snatching the diving pterodactyls right out of the air and smashing them on the sand.

In this place, terror was a familiar state of mind. The daily dose made everything feel like a dreaded chore. Watching the new super-sized raptors making their way toward us, leaving the beach strewn with stunned and staggering pterodactyls and their prey, we were petrified.

Zoe broke our trance.

"Dad," he said, "while I was on the bridge, opening the hatch of the punctured oil hold, I saw that tank number one still has some oil in it. The gauge indicated it was just under a quarter full."

That was all Dad needed to hear. "We've got to blow the ship and escape on the launch," he said. "If there's still some oil in the number one hold, we'll pump it out on deck. Eli, get to the pumps and, on my signal, flood the deck while we roll out the extra barrels of fuel. We'll use the gas to light the oil."

As he spoke, he was jotting down a list of supplies, which he handed to Zoe and Knox.

"Get everything you can into the launch," he ordered. "When the time comes, Zoe, you'll blow the tanks and then join us. I'll work the controls to lower the launch. It might be safer to hide in the superstructure until it's all over, but I for one am not willing to take that chance. We have the means to escape now. Later, that boat out there might be gone."

Dad's reasoning was impeccable. It was also all we had to hear. Survival, while being trapped up here, was an unacceptable alternative. Once again, desperation had taken command, and our plans to separate were dashed.

"Okay, let's *do* it!" Dad shouted.

We scrambled in three directions through the interior passages, while outside on the beach the eating frenzy intensified as the smaller raptors faced off with their larger counterparts.

On the bridge, as I waited for the signal to flood the decks, I could see the giant raptors clearly. They seemed to be planning their next move. As I listened to their clicks and snorts, one turned and glanced my way. It was uncanny to think that they were talking about us. My blood froze as my eyes locked with the reptile's glare, and I was forced to turn away.

My focus returned to the oil hydrants amidships. They had been standing unnoticed until their help was so desperately needed to mix Dad's concoction for life, their twelve-inch spigots silent with their secret. Could they give us the oil we needed to complete this leg of our most perilous plan yet? Everywhere I looked filled me with terror. My body would have collapsed like soft rubber except for the rigid jolt of adrenaline that shot through my core.

Hurry up, you guys! I thought.

As I waited for the signal, praying that the pumps were functional, I wondered how many other things could go wrong before we made our escape.

While Dad and Zoe were busy hooking up the charger to start the lifeboat, Rosario and his men wrestled the drums of fuel onto the weather deck and into position near the open hatches of the first and third oil holds.

Outside on the beach, the action was intensifying. As the

larger raptors attacked the smaller ones, some of them spotted us and began trying to scale the hull, but were not quite able to reach the railing.

Meanwhile, on the stern, things were at a standstill. Our attempts to start the lifeboat were failing. Despite our ability to start the launch the day before, the diesel engine now refused to turn over. Zoe frantically readjusted the jumper cables and pulled the throttle all the way out.

Dad restarted the temperamental generator and prayed to Zoe, "Try it again, son."

Finally, the comatose engine sparked, sputtered, and came to life.

"Alright!" Dad called. "Leave it running while we load this stuff."

Luck was holding for Rosario's detail. Unnoticed by the dinosaurs in all the commotion, his men were rolling the fifty-five gallon drums of gasoline down the deck into position. The first three drums were now standing together by the forward hold. As the men scrambled to complete their task, the noise from the melee on the beach was dreadful. The screeching sounds of claws on metal clashed with the ferocious cacophony as one of the beasts grasped the side railing and pulled itself up on deck. How it ever succeeded in scaling the hull was now irrelevant, but astonishing nonetheless.

"*Jee*-zus!"

Dad had come on the bridge just in time to see the newest development, with Zoe right behind him.

Rosario's men were just about to position the last three drums as the first big raptor stood upright on deck thirty yards away.

"Move, lads!" Knox urged. "Be quick or be dead!"

"Start the pumps now!" Dad yelled to me.

It could have been the charge of energy in his voice that brought those sleeping pumps on line as I threw the switches.

"Green lights!" I cried.

As my eyes stayed glued on those oil spigots standing silent, all hell broke loose.

The ancient sailors ran for the superstructure, their last bastion, but in a few quick strides the monster caught them. Two of the men were gone in a flash—torn, shredded, and devoured. The time it took the beast to tear Wilkes and Villa limb from limb enabled Rosario, Knox, and Joaquin to make it to the door. The enraged lizard never stopped. We were stunned and numb with terror, but there was no time to register our loss, only to keep moving. As the door slammed shut, the black oil flooded the weather deck. Now there were four, then five monsters on deck, ankle deep in free-flowing black crude.

Zoe was up on the second deck, loading the RPG. He threw back the sliding window on the bridge, took aim, and with a steady eye let loose the first salvo. The trusty missile sailed between the nearest raptors and over the second and third holds to its mark. The fulmination lit the entire forward section as the five fifty-gallon drums detonated in quick succession. Zoe put his second shot into the hatchery and his third into the raptor that had taken out Wilkes and Villa. Unlike its victims, the monster never knew what hit him as it toppled over the side. Now Zoe trained on the nearest hold and the remaining drums over the open hatch, firing his last round. This shot would have to do, for there wouldn't be enough time to retrieve the other grenades already packed away on the lifeboat.

As luck would have it, the projectile hit the target but failed to explode. Zoe hadn't counted on the extra round needed for the one that had killed his mates, so he grabbed his Thompson and sprayed the barrels. Gasoline came pouring out of the bullet holes, but didn't ignite. The repeated failures to incinerate the ship and its saurian boarding party had all but sealed our doom, when Zoe reappeared on the weather deck with a flare pistol.

Dad ordered everyone to the stern. "Time to go!" he commanded. "Everybody to the launch!"

At last glance, I saw no less than six jumbos on the forward deck, coming our way. Dad was right—it was now or never. Everyone started for the stern—everyone, that is, except my little brother.

"I'll blow those gas cans," Zoe called, loading the flare gun. "You guys get going. This should do the trick."

While Rosario and his men strapped themselves in on the launch, Dad and I swung it into position. Zoe fired into the stack of gasoline drums, igniting the oil-soaked deck. This set the ship ablaze from superstructure to bow. As the rest of the crude blew up, the creatures went down with ear-splitting screeches that blended with shrieks from the hatchery below.

"Let's go, let's *go!*" Dad shouted, waving frantically at Zoe, who came running around the portside toward the launch.

According to our plan, Dad would be last into the launch after he switched on the winch to lower it away. Zoe scrambled in as it began its descent to the water. The launch was one-third of the way to the waves by the time Dad made it down the guy line and into the enclosed compartment. There wasn't a second to spare as the sea below drew closer.

And then the unthinkable happened—our descent came to an abrupt halt. We were dangling off the fantail twenty feet above the water. After all we had achieved, it was humiliating to be conquered this way.

"What now?" Zoe asked, unbuckling his seatbelt. "The winch must have stalled."

Rosario glared at Dad under his contorted mass of eyebrow and furrowed forehead. "The lines are fouled!" he said. "We're done for!" Then he jumped up from his seat, but realized there was nowhere to go.

Knox, straining in his seatbelt, cried out, "What should we do? We won't last long like this!"

But Dad never quit. "Alright," he said, "we've got to get it running again!"

Above us the tanker had transformed into a funeral pyre for many of the hopeful flesh-eaters as it billowed and blackened the skyline of the insidious jungle, while below us the tumultuous swirling sea awaited. We sat dangling there, awestruck and dumbfounded by this relentless chain of events.

Then Zoe leaped out of his seat and dove through the hatch

for the guy line. "I'll get it," he called.

Normally, there would have been a big discussion about such a perilous task, but we all knew that Zoe was our only chance. In this nightmare, he was a dauntless Tarzan, who excelled in the savage situations that demanded every skill, craft, and trick as payment for each day's existence. Now, with only his hunting knife on his belt, he ascended back into the frying pan in a desperate attempt to keep us out of the fire. Using adrenaline for fuel, he shimmied up the guy line and out of sight.

We sat powerless, dangling for what seemed like hours as some of the nefarious creatures burned, others fought, some ate, and others were eaten.

Our situation was getting worse with each passing moment. At this rate, I was certain the end must be near.

Sure enough, one of the larger raptors spotted us and was wading out toward us. But then I realized this was no raptor. It was a lot bigger—at least twenty-five feet tall.

"Oh, *Jee*-zus, it's Big Bertha!"

Suddenly, the launch jerked and began to lower once again. To me it was like making our first two points when the score was a hundred to nothing. But to give Dad hope, I said, "We're not licked yet!"

He was overwrought, waiting to see Zoe reappear. "Come on, boy," he pleaded to the guy line, "get *down* here!"

Peering out at the gargantuan, I felt that all I had to do was close my eyes, and we would all be in the afterlife.

The beast was only a second away when a wall of water

erupted in front of us. The resulting wake freed the guy line, moving our vessel like a teacup and sending us a good twenty yards away from the stern.

What happened next was almost too much to comprehend as we watched from our limited view. The leviathan had returned. Whatever it was, it was a hundred yards long and came out of the sea with a terrific lurch as it snatched Bertha like an animal cookie in its huge jaws and sank out of sight.

"We're outta here!" Dad shouted with tears streaming down his face. The anguish in his voice was crushing. As he headed full-throttle straight out to sea and toward that ever-present pipe-line, he knew he was eliminating any chance of ever seeing Zoe again.

No one spoke as the launch cut the waves at fifteen knots. Looking ahead, we began to realize that the pipeline was further out than we had thought. The aft porthole view revealed only bellowing black smoke where we had been. However, we could not escape the black gloom within the compartment.

Zoe's absence stripped from me a presence I had relied on all my life, and now a new sense of despair darkened my hori-zon. Life was becoming too much to bear. I could feel the will to survive changing to the desire to end this torturous nightmare at any cost.

The steady drone of the engine was of no comfort as it fanned the embers of hope for escape. We continued unmolested, clos-ing on the last barrier of this unexplainable Bastille.

At first, I thought it was my grief that was chilling me to

the bone. In fact, it was the air inside the compartment that was growing colder.

"*Jee*-zus, I don't know about *this*!" Dad said, speaking for all of us.

It was evident that we had vastly underestimated the size of the pipeline. Penetrating the towering curl and the lightning-streaked pea green curtain would be questionable at best.

"Must be fifty feet high, at least," Dad said. "We'll *never* make that!"

I couldn't believe that Dad was uttering his first words of defeat.

As we got closer, we realized that we had not only misjudged the pipeline's size, but also what it actually was—not a pipeline at all, but a great iceberg that spanned the horizon.

The air temperature continued to drop rapidly.

"How can this be?" Dad said, slowing the boat to a crawl. He was the picture of perplexity, frozen in shock and in disbelief as we crept along toward certain destruction.

"We've arrived at last," railed Rosario, "the very gates of Hell!"

At first, I thought I was seasick when I started to be nauseous and dizzy all at once. Then I heard Dad cry out in pain.

"My back...aaghh!...what's happening?"

As he turned to me, I hardly recognized the face I had gazed on for most of the days of my life. Everything started swimming around me, and something in me already knew what I was trying to come to grips with.

"Dad!" was all that came out of my mouth.

He was looking at me in disbelief.

"My God!" was his reply.

He turned back to the helm, spun the craft around 180 degrees, and pulled the throttle out all the way.

My balance started to return as we moved toward the shore once again. When Dad turned toward me, I realized with horror now that he looked seventy-five years old and totally grey.

"Son," he said to me, "you look like you're fifty. I hardly recognize you."

"What's happened to us, Dad…, what's happening?"

"That may be our answer," he said, pointing behind me to where Rosario, Knox, and Joaquin were strapped in.

I gasped, for three bleached white, clothed skeletons, with skulls back and mouths open, were all that was left of the captain and his men. That feeling of dreaming came over me again, a swimming nausea. I thought I was going to faint.

As I tried to make sense of what was happening to us, the little craft droned on, with Dad never letting go of the wheel.

"We're caught in some kind of time warp," he said at last. "We can't escape, and we can't stay here, either. Our lives have been mutated. This place means to take us out!" Turning to what was left of Rosario and his crew, he said, "I'm sorry…, I was wrong." Then, looking into my eyes, he added, "We've still got each other, and that's enough reason to keep on going."

Dad still had some fight left in him. Once again, his words rescued me from utter despair, focusing me on our duty to each other.

Even so, the loss of Zoe was too much to bear, and we wept openly as the boat made its way back to the circular currents before the breakers. We were five hundred yards offshore when the air temperature returned to what we had been used to.

When Dad shut down the engine, the silence brought me back to the moment as the boat rocked on the rise and fall of the endless swells. Suddenly, Dad and I were the only survivors—if you could call us that. We were mutations of time. My body felt heavy and sluggish.

"Eli," said a voice I hardly recognized, "it's getting dark. We'll drift till morning and hope we don't attract anything in the meantime." Then, moving toward Rosario and his mates, Dad said sadly, "Let's give these sailors their proper burial now before it's dark."

Collecting the remains of our mates was a gruesome task, which we accomplished in silence, putting one foot in front of the other, doing what had to be done. After a brief but solemn service, we let the three ancient mariners drift down into Davy Jones's locker.

Darkness soon overtook us, as did our grief.

Of all the fierce denizens in this Paleolithic sea, surely something will find us and end our misery.

This was my prayer.

As the night passed, the gentle rocking of the boat finally lulled us to sleep.

IV

Bright sunshine pierced through my dreams. Proof that I had slept. But then reality slammed me into full consciousness. I felt miserable. In one devastating day, we had aged twenty years and lost Zoe.

He's gone!

Dad was still asleep. As I looked at him, I thought of the grandfather I never knew. When I passed him on my way out on deck, he started to wake. Gazing at the shore, I saw that we were still a good five hundred yards out. The beach didn't have any recognizable features. The mountain, the Wizard's Hat, shot out of the jungle canopy, and at the moment, this island in Hell looked like a postcard.

Then I saw it. As usual, the laser beam—or whatever it was—was shooting out of the mountaintop. I did a double take when I realized that this *wasn't* as usual. Up until now, the beam had only been visible at night. This morning it was visible in the sunlight.

When Dad came on deck, I pointed out the change.

"We've been pondering that thing long enough," he said. "Now it even beckons to us in the daytime. Let's head for it."

Returning to the helm, he brought the engine to life, swung the boat around, and headed in. We were three hundred yards out and closing when a bay came into view.

"There's an inlet at one o'clock," I called.

"I see it."

We made way toward the fifteen-foot breakers that we would have to negotiate a hundred yards offshore. These waves were picture-perfect with a rip curl pipeline, each one an expressway to the beach—if you knew the trick.

Dad knew the trick. He eased the little shuttle into the swell and used the engine to match the wave's speed, causing the boat to leap ahead, energized by the full momentum of the perfect wave.

What a ride! The little boat was a third out of the water as we surfed that endless curl right into the middle of the bay.

Dad cut the engine. No need to waste gas. In the direction of the mountain, there was a river big enough to fit the boat.

Then I remembered the map on Themi's bowl. We still had Themi's side sack. Zoe had loaded it along with his other prize possessions, the two Thompsons and the RPG.

"Themi's bowl showed a river on it," I said. "Maybe this is it."

"Maybe it is, maybe not," said Dad. "Regardless, I'd rather stay in the boat as long as we can, so I guess we're going upriver.

But let's stay here and out of sight until tomorrow. I'm not feeling ready to go on yet."

Dad was already tired. I could hear it in his voice. I missed the vigor that was no longer there. Gone was the aggressive enthusiasm that always accompanied his plans. In its place was a tone of listless avoidance.

I opened a tin of beef stew, which Dad and I shared, leaving most of it uneaten. After that, we fell back to sleep for hours.

When I woke up, the sun had set and its crimson afterglow was fading fast. Dad was up, but wasn't moving around much. He was still sitting where he had slept.

The little boat rocked gently on the once mighty swells as they dissipated into this moonlit bay. In the silence of our grief, darkness fell over us unnoticed. The fight had gone out of us. With no foreseeable hope for escape, there was no reason to rush on. Our curiosity about the mountain was overshadowed by grief.

And so another night passed. Although slumber was intermittent at best, there weren't any unsettling interruptions, and we were sound asleep when the sun came up.

Dad heard it first and shook me awake. Unmistakably, we were being boarded. When the hatch slid open, we couldn't believe our eyes! The dark silhouette was a familiar one.

"Dad...? Eli...?"

"Zoe!"

We were frozen, awestruck with a joy that dissolved our grief. Zoe was alive and peering into our darkened compartment.

He heard us before he saw us.

"Yeah, it's me!" he said.

More than a happy ending, this was a miracle! A tsunami of emotion overtook us as we came to realize that Zoe was alive, and we were all still together. For a moment, our mutations were forgotten, but as we made our way forward, the daylight caught us, Dad first, then me.

Zoe reeled back, trying to comprehend what he was seeing. His expression was one I had never seen in all our years together. He was aghast.

"What...what happened? It's you, Dad..., Eli! God, what happened?"

"It's us, son," Dad said, his voice cutting through Zoe's confusion. "What happened is that you're not dead, and neither are we. We're together again, thank God. That's all that really matters. We're still in this place with its freaky eddies of time, and we've been mutated by it somehow. Anyway, right now we're together again, and that means more to me than anything we've been through."

Wet, haggard, and fatigued, Zoe had evidently been tested by endurance since we had last seen him. Dirty and smelly, scraped and scratched, he all but collapsed as his adrenaline subsided. Sinking into a chair, he devoured the beef stew that we had left over. Then we all celebrated with a tin of peaches. Between swallows, Zoe told us the story of his grueling escape.

"Just after I got the winch working again," he said, "I was swept overboard by the wake of the sea beasts as they took each other out. The wave swept me forward and over the side, landing me in a pile of dino dung. That turned out to be my salvation. To my surprise, my new stench qualified me as an untouchable, and I was able to get away from that hot spot in Hell. Without getting much sleep since then, I made my way over the cliffs, where I saw the mountain's beam in the daytime. I was moving up the beach with first light when I came upon this bay and you guys."

As he told us his story, Zoe tried not to show how our new appearance was affecting him. All that mattered was that we were together again.

We told him how we had aged and how Rosario, Knox, and Joaquin had met their end.

"I'm sorry they're gone," he said. "In our short time with them, we all went through a lot together. I'll miss them."

As Zoe fell into a deep sleep, Dad and I decided to stay in the bay another day before continuing on to whatever was waiting for us on the mountain. This little bay was like a sanctuary.

The next morning, Dad was talking with Zoe as I came on deck.

"Ever since we first discovered it," he was saying, "everything has been pointing us toward that beam."

"Yes," Zoe said, "I see that now..., so let's not fight it. Let's find out what it has in store for us."

"It seems to be the only way left to go," I said.

As Zoe turned to me, it was obvious that he was still unsettled by my aged features. Trying not to notice, he continued, "The beam is due north from here. I took a bearing when I first saw it."

It was midday by the time we got started, wending our way down this river, which inexplicably flowed in from the sea. We couldn't explain the reverse current any more than we could explain the massive ice barrier on the horizon or the sharp contrast in temperature between there and here.

Before long, the steaming jungle swallowed us up. There was no shortage of chilling soloists in the ravenous denizens' choir. Since the current was moving the boat fast enough for us to navigate, we decided to cut the engine.

Then Dad came up with a theory about the ice barrier.

"Maybe," he said, "it's somehow in a different time. As we approached it, we may have actually been passing through ripples in time, which would explain how we became older."

It was a strange working theory, but we couldn't think of anything other than that far-fetched explanation. Like this river that flowed inland from the sea, it defied reason, but there it was.

We were in the middle of the winding river, with twenty to thirty yards of water on each side of us. The densely foliated shoreline was overburdened with lush blooms of rarely seen exotic hues, but from time to time it was bare. We were moving along at two or three knots, keeping in the middle of the river as we made our way toward the ominous mountain.

"This is why the man in the boat on Themi's bowl has his arms folded," I said. "He doesn't have to paddle."

"According to the story the bowl told us on the tanker," Zoe said, "if this is that river, we should soon come to the mountain. Anyway, we're traveling in the right direction, don't you think?" When we didn't answer, he turned to us. "*Jee*-zus!" He was using Dad's alarm word.

There on the port side stood a golden saber-toothed cat. It was huge—five feet tall, a good seven feet long, and snarling a bloodcurdling roar as it stalked us along our way. The water was our ally once again as it kept our latest tormentor away. As long as the river stayed this wide, it seemed we were further out than he was willing to go for lunch.

Surveying our position, Dad said, "Hope this river stays nice and wide. Ten minutes into the trip, and already we've got trouble."

As we continued on in silence, the perpetual echoes of hunger rang through the jungle, and now it was the giant cat that dominated the chorus.

"We need to open up the boat to get some room to fight," Zoe said. He never liked being enclosed. "The hood blocks our view and our ability to respond if that cat gives us a shot at him."

We did as Zoe suggested, sliding the telescopic sections fore and aft into the center.

Zoe called to me, "Get the Thompsons and some ammo!"

When I returned with the ordnance, we had another surprise. Now there was a second giant saber-tooth. The creature saw us in the same instant that we saw it, acknowledging us with a paralyzing roar, much louder than that of its companion. As it reared back on its hind legs at the water's edge, Zoe nimbly loaded both machine guns. Pulling back the bolts, he clicked the safeties, then lay one gun down for me and slung the other over his shoulder. The cats were working together as they ran up and down on the shoreline, trying to find a way around their dislike for water. It must have been dislike, for fear could not have been a part of their repertoire.

Dad was keeping us in the middle, but Zoe wasn't satisfied.

"Better get out the RPG for backup," he said. "We'll probably need everything if we need anything!"

Moments later, I was laying out the launcher and our last five grenades for quick and easy access.

Thinking of our diminishing arsenal, Zoe said, "We won't shoot unless we absolutely have to, which could be any minute."

The river turned lazily—right, then left. The cats stood glowering, their spastic switching tails signaling their frustration as we floated through their domain. They followed our progress all afternoon, sometimes out of sight, but always snarling their intentions each time they reestablished visual contact. Unseen, their vicious roars and snarling continued to dominate the incessant feral chorus. Another twenty minutes passed with no new developments. Our stalkers were relentless, and our nerves were wearing thin.

Zoe's machine gun was in his hands once again, fingers massaging the safety as he spoke. "Maybe we should hook up and get moving instead of drifting along like this."

"I don't know," Dad said. "That might get a bad reaction from them if they thought their monkey pie was getting away."

Considering this possibility, Zoe nodded.

"Let's play this out for a while longer," Dad said, trying as usual to be optimistic. "Maybe they'll give up and go home."

Zoe shot me a quick smirk. "They *are* home, Dad."

Ancient towering trees with long thick hanging vines were everywhere. There were throngs of monkeys, the first we had seen in this jungle, and flocks of brilliantly colored parrots and cockatoos, along with many other species of larger fowl, all intent on their own survival. The pungent canopy towered over us on both sides, creating deep shadows with intermittent shafts of golden light. As we came around another bend, the river narrowed, but still kept us out of reach of the hydrophobic saber-tooths, who had become quiet. After another turn toward the mountain, we could no longer feel their presence, their familiar voices now totally absent from the perpetual din. This was all the excuse we needed to feel some relief.

Suddenly, the boat took an unnatural but familiar sideways movement. No one spoke—we didn't have to. The last time we had felt a countermovement like that was when the leviathan was passing under the outrigger. As one, we leaned over the side and peered into the rippling green water. That's when we saw the whole thing. Its long bony head was the size of a large table, followed by many feet of the fattest serpent this river could ever house. We froze as the green and orange striped creature slithered beneath us.

"*Jee*-zus!" Dad whispered. "It's a snake or giant eel. And it's going in the same direction we are. It's lucky we didn't start the engine back there. I don't think it knows we're here."

A horrified silence was our only response. We all kept our thoughts to ourselves as we continued to drift along with the current, while the sun left the sky and darkness overtook another day in this nightmare jungle.

"Look at *that!*" Dad whispered in the twilight, pointing toward the two feline stalkers, who were keeping their distance from the water's edge as they watched us slip away. "I guess now we know why the water's off limits to them."

Knowing that the vile river serpent was somewhere up ahead, we kept still and said no more. The canopy was too thick to see the mountain, but the boat's compass said we were on course as we drifted along, ever vigilant.

Finally, we came to a place that was wide enough to drop anchor. The sounds of the river provided us with enough cover to hide our restricted noises. As usual, there were unexplained sounds in the night and a few weird shifts in the boat's position, but we knew what all small creatures know: keep quiet, don't move, and maybe trouble will go away.

The last thing I remember was thinking it would be impossible to sleep in this seething racket. But we were exhausted and soon fell into a deep, replenishing slumber.

With first light, we got under way, drifting lazily along in the contrary current toward the Wizard's Hat.

"It can't be much farther," I speculated. "We should see it

by noon."

By mid-morning, we had made continuous unmolested progress. Themi's bowl had indicated that we should come to a junction any time now.

Dad had fallen back to sleep beneath the enclosed section amidships. I was on the tiller, and Zoe was next to me, cleaning his weapon, when, all of a sudden, the river serpent was back. Its rapacious head and twenty feet of mean body came rising up silently before us just ten feet off the port bow. Looming above us, threatening to strike, it seemed to be cursing us, hissing its cruel intent, its vile snarl revealing fangs that could impale. The unspoken moment we were dreading was at hand.

I was paralyzed, but hard as I tried, I couldn't speak.

Stepping out of the enclosure, Zoe reacted matter-of-factly, aiming his grenade launcher as he said softly, "Hold it steady."

I was frozen at the tiller, but Zoe's wish was my command. The wretched reptile glared at us, its lizard-like mouth opened wider, and, hissing venomously, it came for us. Zoe let loose. The well-placed round looked like a cough drop as the beast swallowed it, just as the raptor had done that morning when we were attacked in the Martin Mariner. I thought I saw a look of surprise come over our tormentor just before his head exploded. What was left of the serpent fell back and sank out of sight as we passed over where it had been.

"Well, at least that one won't be bothering us anymore," Zoe said in an effort to ease our sense of vulnerability.

I was still speechless, but thankful. The explosion woke Dad, but he was only annoyed. By the time he focused in, all traces of the incident had vanished.

Sitting up, he looked around and scolded us, "What's all the noise about? Be quiet…before we get company we don't want!"

"Sorry, Dad," was all Zoe said.

I looked at Zoe but said nothing. Already dozing off again, Dad was oblivious to what had just happened. If the situation hadn't been so desperate, it would have been comical. Instead, seeing this old and tired side of Dad was unnerving.

He sat up again in afterthought. "And don't waste ammo…. *Jee*-zus!"

As Dad continued to nap, several uneventful hours passed before we intersected with a larger river.

Zoe broke the silence: "Hey, we're coming to the mountain."

This junction confirmed our theory about the bowl being a map of the mountain with a message we had yet to decipher. Now the river was running alongside the mysterious volcano. As indicated by Themi's map, it followed the massive cone like the brim of a hat. The mountain rose up out of the water in sheer cliffs along most of the shoreline. Then the river widened as we came to cascading waterfalls. Falling from some fifty feet above, the water column plummeted unobstructed into the river.

Awake now, Dad was tuned into the moment. We were deep in the jungle, where the denizens' racket was as jarring as ever. My jagged nerves tugged at my stomach as we made our way to—we knew not what. Our apprehension was high and our morale low. No one wanted to acknowledge that the future looked dim at best.

As if to accentuate our dismal circumstance, dark storm clouds started to block the sun, replacing with a grey mantle what had been a bright sunny day only moments before. The sultry stillness of the jungle air vanished. It was getting colder by the minute.

The falls were now behind us, almost out of sight, when Zoe yelled, "On deck! Get ready to pull in, there's something coming up!" When he turned the key, the boat lurched forward. Then, looking at the shore, he said, "How can this be?"

The prolific overgrowth left only a portion of it exposed, but it was still recognizable.

"I'd know that saucer anywhere," Zoe said, standing ready to leap ashore with a tie line. "Somehow, Dad," he said, "I think this is the same one. Let's check it out." He jumped onto the shore and pulled us in with the rope as the temperature continued to drop.

The saucer wasn't visible from where we tied up. Dad wanted to be sure there weren't any giant cats around before we did anything else. Armed with two Thompsons and one machete, we remained silent, anticipating our next encounter.

Throngs of monkeys chattered above us as they scampered through the trees, which we interpreted as a sign that there was no immediate danger.

"Let's go to see the saucer while we can," Zoe said, starting toward it, slashing his way through the dense undergrowth. "It's right over there."

We followed behind, more than a little spooked and watching out for attacks from every direction.

"How can this be the same craft we saw under water?" I asked. "No real way of telling, but I would bet that at least this one was made in the same flying saucer factory."

"No doubt about it," said Zoe. "It's the same saucer-type craft we saw the day this all began."

Nearly invisible under a heavy overgrowth, except for its south side, the saucer was big, about two hundred feet in diameter and eighteen feet high. The hull was smooth and unscathed. Our minds raced with images of what might have been its story. There were Egyptian-like symbols around the midsection, decorating a six-foot-high golden band, below which there was an obvious entryway. Except for the jungle overgrowth, there was no indication of how old the craft was or how long it had been here like this.

And there was something else.

"Not good!" I said, pointing to the immense paw prints where we were standing.

Their distinct impression in the rich black earth proclaimed the perils involved in this reconnaissance.

"Paw prints," Zoe said. "Large, cat-like...more than one or two came through here not long ago!" Although he read the tracks like an eviction notice, Zoe seemed oblivious to the perils of our situation as he threw himself into his work.

I no longer felt the extra weight of the Thompson, although it was hard to focus on the exploration when every instinct was telling me to keep my eyes on the obscure perimeter of the jungle maze.

"Maybe there's an open entry on the other side," Zoe said, vigorously hacking away at the foliage.

"So far, so good," Dad said, "but let's not press our luck out here too much longer."

A few days before, we wouldn't have been able to hold Dad back from a complete recon on our first encounter, but he no longer had the stamina or drive.

"Okay, Dad," Zoe said, "just a little more, and we'll quit for today." He was hacking away at some tall ferns as he continued around the perimeter of the strange craft. "There might be some more clues to all this just a little farther on."

"This is enough for today, son. It'll be dark soon. Let's get back to the boat and batten down. We'll freeze out here before much longer."

Something in Dad's tone snapped Zoe out of it. He stopped mid-swing and lowered his machete. We were all shivering, our scant clothing offering no protection.

"Yeah, you're right, Dad," Zoe conceded. "Tomorrow's another day…, I hope."

As we turned around, I took point, with Dad and Zoe following behind. The saucer had come close to smashing into the sheer side of the Wizard's Hat. We tried to speculate on whether the landing was controlled or lucky, but so far there weren't any definite indications of a crash landing.

Then, pointing to an opening twenty feet up the sheer side of the mountain, Dad called, "Up there! Looks like a perfect triangle."

"Yeah," I agreed. "Like the ones on the bowl."

There were three concentric triangles on Themi's bowl, one inside the other. The one on the mountainside appeared to be a single perfect triangle forming the opening of a cave.

"That might be what we're looking for," Dad said. "We'll check it out first thing tomorrow. Let's go!"

Somewhere in the Stygian jungle, a big cat roared. But this one was different. It sounded like a lion. His horrific promise reverberated beneath the canopy. Fear, ranging from general paranoia to stark terror, was a daily condition in this vicious world of predators and paradox.

I wondered how much longer our quest for survival could last. Lately, it seemed I was always afraid. Also, my heart was heavy with a deep concern for Dad.

As the sun started to set, we only had a short hike back to the boat. Dad perked up as the river came into view.

"There's the boat," he cried. "Home!"

We were a motley crew, making our way back to the river, mutated by time and lost in some reality that was not our own. Our morale dwindled with every step—and then things got worse.

"*Jee*-zus!"

There were two of them—full-grown lions, positioned in front of the small clearing where the boat was tied. We stood motionless as four more of the biggest cats I had ever seen joined the first two. Each one was six feet high and eight feet long. With their tails quivering, they were sniffing the ground and the rope from the boat.

"They'll get our scent!" I whispered. The very thought sent a jolt of terror through me.

"We won't be going home tonight, boys," Dad said. "Let's head for that cave up there."

With Thompsons at the ready, we backed out of our observation point and made tracks for the mountain. Dad struggled to keep a quick pace, but he was tiring fast.

"We'll rest for a minute," Zoe said, stopping under a large bole.

"We can't stay," Dad said, breathing hard. "We've gotta keep moving."

Zoe stood by Dad, gun at the ready. "Just two minutes," he said, "and we'll move out again."

Dad didn't protest.

The tone of the monkeys' chatter high up in the trees suddenly changed. Now they seemed to be scolding us, or maybe they were egging us on. Whichever it was, their incessant racket only added to our apprehension. This part of the jungle was splotched with small clearings and profuse vegetation.

All at once it went quiet. The ever-present din ceased, and the hairs on the back of my neck stood on end. We knew from years of playing paintball that it was too quiet.

Too quiet means ambush!

Out of the impenetrable thicket came earsplitting, bloodcurdling roars as the cats sprang on us from three sides. The first lion startled Zoe, who reeled back off balance, but his finger squeezed the trigger, and his attacker took the full blast of the Thompson's barrage. Zoe followed the monster to the ground before his finger let up. Another leaped out in front of me, just behind Dad. I let loose and the big cat spun to face me as a wave of hot lead took him down. I heard Zoe's gun again as I realized that he was still too busy to cover Dad. Just then, yet another lion came leaping out of the jungle foliage to my right. Turning away from Dad, I released another wall of hot lead until it fell. Then both guns fell silent.

"Dad!" Zoe called. His cry was agonizing.

When I swung around, I saw my brother climbing over one of four dead lions that surrounded him. He was frantic. I looked around for Dad. Converging on where he should have been, Zoe and I stared at the knife that Dad had been carrying and the trail of blood that led off through the brush.

"Let's go!" Zoe yelled. "Hurry, they can't be far!"

He was right. As we came to a small clearing, we stopped dead in our tracks. The cats were fighting among themselves. The biggest one went unmolested as he gorged himself. I was numb, my thoughts liquefying as my heart sank irretrievably. The unthinkable had happened. Dad was gone, and the other lions were waiting for their share of what was left of him.

Zoe had had enough. "Let's end this nightmare right here and now, Eli," he sobbed. With tears streaming, he turned the Thompson on himself. "This is too much to take."

"No, Zoe!" I shouted, grabbing the weapon from him. "I'm not gonna lose you, too. C'mon, we've gotta keep trying. It's what Dad would have expected us to do. C'mon, Dad is keeping them busy while we make our break. Let's go!" I grabbed his arm and shook him. "Come on, Bro, don't let me die here!"

Zoe got a new grip on the moment. "Okay, Eli, let's go," he said, taking back his Thompson. "We'll try to make the cave up there."

He looked back once more, but I didn't. As we headed toward the mountain, we stopped for a breather by the saucer. It was starting to rain, a cold, penetrating downpour.

"Just what we need! How much more can we take?" Zoe was speaking for both of us. "If it weren't for that cave, I'd say we were at trail's end. Looks like about twenty yards to the mountain."

He had his machete out, and I kept guard as we pressed on.

"How much ammo do you have left, Eli?" he asked.

"One clip and about eight loose," I said.

Zoe stopped slashing the brush. "I'm almost out.... I used everything except one or two shots."

"Hey, it ain't over till it's over," I said, trying to sound positive.

As if to mock my words, the torrential rain turned to sleet.

"At this rate," Zoe said, "we'll be frozen by nightfall!"

He wasn't being sarcastic; the temperature was continuing to plummet. Once again, it was pure adrenaline that kept us going. We heard the lions roaring not very far off. Zoe started slashing once again as I kept my eyes peeled for any movement. We were progressing slowly through the dense undergrowth when we came close enough to see our objective clearly.

The cave was surely man-made. Its lines were sharp and deliberate, a perfect triangle. A few more yards and we would be climbing the icy rocks that led to the ominous opening.

"Here they come!" Zoe yelled, as he slashed viciously through the last few yards. "Choose your shots!"

The first cat appeared ten yards behind us and closing fast. I responded with two short bursts, and then my gun went silent with a click.

"Loading!" I shouted, slamming in the last clip and pulling back the bolt.

There were growls of fury and agony as the ferocious feline thrashed about in its death throes. Another lion appeared and jumped over the downed leader. I repeated the sequence, and it fell, too.

"Over there," Zoe said, pointing at the rock formation near the cave.

There were four more lions between us and our objective. When they came at us, Zoe fired his last two shots. His target veered and ran off, wounded. I sprayed the remaining three, hitting at least two as they also veered from their course and disappeared into the brush.

Throwing down his Thompson, Zoe yelled, "Let's go!"

While the predators regrouped, we scampered up the outcropping of rock. It was a four-foot leap to the cave opening from the top of the rock formation. The sleet changed into a driving snowstorm and then a full-scale blizzard. Our whole environment was now focused as a single force intent on ending our lives, but we were relentless.

"This will give me incentive," Zoe said, throwing his machete into the dark opening that was our only hope for escape.

He jumped across, making it with barely an inch to spare. Now it was my turn.

"I'll toss my Thompson over first," I said.

Zoe nodded, putting his hands out to catch it. But I lost my balance, slipped, and fell the six feet down to the ground. The fall knocked the wind out of me, but I wasn't hurt.

"Here they come!" Zoe called, just in time for me to recover my gun and aim at another lion that was trying to finish me off. Once again, the trusty Thompson came through. But this was the noble weapon's last act. The ammo was gone.

"C'mon!" shouted Zoe from above.

I was up and climbing as I saw another lion coming toward me. This time I got to the jump-off point, leaped to the cave, and fell into Zoe's waiting arms.

"Let's go!" I said.

As I rolled off Zoe, I was pounced on. The beast was intent. I could feel its hot, foul breath as it came in for the kill. Once again, my brother saved my life, driving his machete deep with a thrust through the neck and down into the heart. The big cat fell away with Zoe's machete still lodged in its flesh. For a moment, it contorted violently, then relaxed.

"We're weaponless now, Eli," Zoe said. "Move, move, move!"

He pulled me to my feet and pushed me toward the back of the cave. But we weren't out of trouble yet. Another lion crawled up the rocks, belly to the ground, its tail twitching nervously, and then suddenly, with a vicious roar, charged to make the leap across.

"Keep going!" Zoe shouted.

We moved some twenty feet to the back of the cave until we came to another triangular opening, this one about half the height of the cave's entrance. We tumbled through and proceeded another twenty feet. In the dim half-light, all we could see was a faint golden glow coming from a third triangular opening, which looked too small to crawl through. Now it was almost pitch dark as our pursuer blocked the light from outside, snarling in expectation of its prize.

I urged Zoe on. "Keep going, Bro!"

Zoe crawled into the tight hole, and I followed.

"What a way to go," he lamented. "We're trapped!"

The thing he hated most was close quarters. Claustrophobia was his Achilles heel.

"I don't think they can fit into this hole," I said. "We may be safe for the moment."

"I can't stand it in tight spaces like this," Zoe yelled. "I can't do this! I can't *stand* it!"

"We're not trapped, Zoe. There's light ahead. Take it easy and keep going! Look, see that? There's light! Keep going, keep going!"

He did as I said, and we crawled another twenty feet or so. Then the light started getting brighter. In another ten feet, the ceiling started to rise, and we could stand once again.

The big cat was furious. His roar was deafening, but it was the only part of him that the third triangle would allow to pass.

It was warm here, a lot warmer than outside. Even though we were soaked to the bone, we were warm again, and that felt good.

After walking a little farther, we came upon a breathtaking sight—a human bust carved out of the rock. Glowing softly, a pulsating amber light emanated from within, enhancing the expression on the face, which appeared familiar and friendly. Behind the sculpture flowed a stream, which cascaded down the wall within the volcano and then split into several waterfalls before continuing its descent to the crater floor. The water was cold and clear. After a long drink, we were considerably refreshed.

"There it is!" Zoe cried, pointing off into the distance at the familiar laser-like beam shooting straight up.

There was no doubt about it. We were inside the Wizard's Hat. Looking up, we had a circular view of the starry sky. It was obvious that the crater was vast. There in the darkness, we could see little else. Even now that we were inside the immense crater, we could only see the laser-like shaft of light. It was too dark to see its point of origin, which was somewhere beneath us. It was also too dark to venture on. We decided to stay put until first light.

As our adrenaline subsided, we were overtaken by fatigue and heartbreak. Lying down next to the pulsating sculpture, we soon lapsed into a deep sleep.

I awoke bathed in the same amber light that had been emanating from the sculpture. Zoe was up and gazing out across the vast crater's floor in the morning light. Now we could see where the ominous laser beam came from. It shot out from the top of a pyramid on the crater floor. Around it was a village surrounded by furrowed fields and a winding river.

With tears in his eyes, Zoe said, "This place was calling to us the whole time. I wish Dad could've seen it."

The immense crater basked in the golden sunlight from above. An inexplicable all-present amber glow hung everywhere in this hidden paradise. We stood there awestruck, unaware that we were not alone.

"*Chi sono voi?*"

A sweet uplifting voice was asking us in Italian who we were.

We spun around, and saw standing before us a strikingly beautiful young woman. She had black hair and eyes like piercing pools of midnight. Her white wrap revealed her supple breasts. As she stood waiting for our answer, Zoe's mouth dropped, but he quickly regained his composure.

"Must be paradise," Zoe answered softly, also in Italian.

With no indication of hearing Zoe's comment, our vision spoke again. "I don't know you," she said. "Who are you, my brothers? Where did you come from?" Her tone had a touch of attitude that snapped us out of our trance.

"My name is Zoroaster, and this is my brother Elias. We were shipwrecked not far from here."

Zoe's answers seemed curt to me and strange to her as she stared at him with a quizzical gaze. Preoccupied with her appearance, Zoe was unaware of his abbreviated delivery.

"We were chased by lions," he added, "escaping through the cave that leads here."

Her gaze continued as she tried to understand his explanation. Zoe spoke fluent Italian, so there was no language barrier. It was *what* he was saying that gave her alluring face the tilt of incomprehension.

"Who are you?" I asked. "What is this place called?"

A comely smile replaced the hint of perplexity on her face. "I am Shakti," she said. "I live here in this mountain…, the Wizard's Hat."

I decided against bringing up Themi's fate just yet.

"How is it…how is it possible," I stammered, "that this place is so bountiful and beautiful and…, and this lighting…, how is it possible?"

Realizing the fragmented state of my question, I let it stand. Smiling, Shakti seemed to comprehend. But my query went unanswered as we were joined by a group of three men and two women. They looked wholesome, with strong bodies and a gentle manner. As Shakti reported our situation to them, they seemed to have been expecting us. Their eyes never left us as they talked among themselves. Their gaze was not threatening in any way, and at no time did I feel anything but warm sensitivity from them. A nod of agreement and their conference was over.

One of the men turned to us and said with a smile, "You must be hungry. Go with Shakti. She will feed you."

All this time, Zoe hadn't said a word. I could see that he had relapsed into sadness over Dad.

Starting down the winding path, Shakti turned and signaled us to follow. Everything about this mountain goddess served to draw us in. I think we would have followed her anywhere.

As we walked along, I asked her to explain what was happening to us.

"Where are we?" I asked. "What is this island called? How have we come to be here in this prehistoric environment?"

She turned around and said with a smile, "We had no choice. We had to run the experiment that has brought you here. I'll take you to my mother for your questions. She will have questions for you as well. And food…, plenty of good food."

Her words felt intimate, as if we were part of her family. As we continued down the path, I wondered what we would discover about these gentle people, who spoke Italian so beautifully.

Was that their flying saucer outside? Is Zoe going to be alright? He seems too quiet.

The pastoral grandeur of this enchanting habitat was

compelling. Now the path started across to the crater floor toward a river that rolled and curled through this ethereal garden. Never had we seen such natural splendor, almost too beautiful for words, all set in a massive dormant volcano. The contrast of this place with the world outside was like stepping from the gates of hell into paradise. But it was also like a battle dressing on an open wound. Taking it all in created a euphoric feeling, but there was nothing to tend to the bottomless loss that had us feeling so hopelessly broken. That we were weaponless was of little concern to us.

Breaking his morose silence, Zoe said in English, "I wish Dad could have seen this."

I didn't respond. My severe sense of loss had left me in a state of numb acceptance.

Soon we arrived at a river with a hemp footbridge, which swayed ten feet above the rapids as we crossed in single file. Beyond the bridge, the path widened into a long street that ended at the foot of the pyramid. There were more dwellings, two- and three-story pueblos on both sides of the boulevard. Now we could see that all the streets ran in concentric circles around the pyramid. I imagined that the village must look like a bull's-eye target from above. The spacious dwellings had an elegance that felt homey and friendly.

Suddenly, a drum started to beat out a steady rhythm. Then another drum echoed the first, and then another.

Feeling Zoe's despondency, Shakti took his arm in hers as we continued walking. Zoe accepted her gesture with a faint smile.

"Soon everyone will know you are here," she said. Her words gave us a glimmer of hope.

Shakti's warm grip on Zoe's arm improved his state of mind. As a new drum rang out above the others, she turned to us and stopped, her eyes widening as she listened to the drum repeating itself. When she looked directly into Zoe's eyes, the color returned to his face.

"The drums say you are brothers from our future," she said, "brought here as a result of the experiment."

The nature of this experiment remained elusive to us, but she spoke of it as something her people had no choice in.

Zoe shrugged. "Perhaps that's the answer to this sleepless nightmare."

Shakti tightened her grip on his arm.

"What's the experiment about?" I asked. "And where is it being performed?"

Glancing at me to answer, she said, "My mother is old and wise. She may have the answers you seek. We're almost there."

This utopian environment conveyed a feeling of enchantment. Acres of pastoral and park-like landscape replete with orchards surrounded the circular village of elegant gardens and comfortable dwellings. There was an uncanny sense of familiarity in all of this. Everyone acknowledged us as we passed, and I waved back with affection for these gracious and friendly souls.

"This way," Shakti said, gesturing toward a serene and cozy dwelling at the end of a path of turquoise steppingstones. A profuse multicolored explosion of flowers served as a hedgerow on both sides of the ample approach. Shakti walked to the doorless entry of the two-story dwelling and stepped inside. As we followed her, she stood next to another young woman, who was reclining on a Romanesque couch covered with golden furs.

"Mother," Shakti said, "these men are the brothers Elias and Zoroaster." Then, turning to us, she said, "I would like you to meet my mother. Her name is Cristal."

We were taken aback when Shakti introduced this young woman as her mother. High cheekbones gave her face a regal, ageless beauty, and even though she seemed taller than Shakti, she appeared to be no more than two or three years older. Maybe their sense of time was different. It seemed like a prank that we were supposed to believe that these two young women were mother and daughter. On the other hand, the two of us must have looked like father and son to them.

"You are welcome here," Cristal said. "Come in." Her voice was soothing, her words like kisses from home.

The room was simply furnished with elegant pieces, including a large round oak table, low to the ground but graceful and sturdy, with scrollwork in a sunburst design.

Cristal motioned for all of us to sit down on the couches around the table.

As soon as we were seated, young food bearers brought us water and then a large platter of spicy meat over a grain that resembled brown rice. Next, several bowls of grapes and other fruits, nuts, and bread were placed before us. I wondered if the servers were Shakti's brothers and sisters. Whoever these people were, they observed the same wonderful customs of hospitality toward strangers as did the ancient Greeks. Shakti's mother was as gracious as she was beautiful. Her infatuating smile exuded hospitality.

"Please take this food and refresh yourselves," she said. "There will be plenty of time for talk afterward."

The effect of everything that had happened was swelling up within me. As Cristal spoke, I realized how long it had been since our last meal.

"Thank you, we are very hungry," was all I could say.

Zoe seconded my statement with an appreciative nod as he tore at his bread. In no time, we devoured nearly everything. I had never tasted fruit so sweet. Even the nuts were especially rich.

Shakti kept her dark saucer eyes on Zoe as he ate. But when she noticed me watching her, she looked away. Oblivious to the moment's potential, Zoe went on eating. It had been a long time since we had felt the snug contentment of an excellent meal.

As our eating frenzy subsided, Cristal said, "My daughter tells me you have questions. Perhaps I can answer them. There are questions we have for you as well."

As she said this, a swarm of questions came to mind. Where would I begin? *What about the flying saucer? Better not hit that one first. What's your story? What's your secret? Why do you speak Italian? How long has this been going on?* A myriad of questions raced through one fleeting moment, and then I began.

"You must know," I said, "how you came to be here in this place. My brother and I don't know where we are. Perhaps you can tell us who your people are and where you come from?"

My question echoed in my ears as I waited for an answer.

Cristal looked at us lovingly as she spoke. "Whatever the explanation for your present situation, certain things remain true. Whoever you are and whoever we are, we are of the same family. We are all brothers and sisters, the children of the Creator and heirs to all creation."

Her warm explanation was more than familiar. This was the same philosophy that Dad had taught us all our lives. I wanted to hear more.

"We are not from this world," she continued. "We came here to Atlantis from Eden on the garden planet of Lamoria. Once in every hundred thousand generations, there travels on the solar winds that beloved cosmic creeper known as Mankind. Once in every Age of Man, there comes a generation of humans that set out from their garden planet guided by the enlightenment of the Esseen Crystals in search of the next sweet spot in the Universe, where the conditions are right to germinate yet another Eden. There have been countless Ages of Man in which this wonderful process has brought about their divine fruition. Occasionally, an attempt may be hindered in one way or another. Such was *our* fate. However, we have survived and are determined to complete our mission to make this planet another Eden. Our crystals keep us healthy and provide for all our needs. Their light properties create these lush gardens and orchards as well as allowing us to live in the prime of life almost indefinitely. That is, aging is a very slow process for us."

For a fleeting instant, the possibility that we had expired and that this was heaven ran through my bewilderment. As all this unraveled into my consciousness, I could see and feel the connection between this place and our oldest legends and myths of Adam and Eve and of Atlantis. It gave me a warm feeling that replenished my spirit. The way she shared her people's story like this made me feel genuinely welcome and loved.

Our hosts sang and played enthralling songs, telling stories that described their home world and their journey through the cosmos in search of the next Garden of Eden. Euphonious tones emanated softly from an array of winds, strings, and percussion instruments, including tambourines. These sensuous sounds prevailed all through the evening as musicians joined in from among those present.

But even with the effect of these extraordinary revelations, Zoe could not stop thinking about Dad, and was forced to mask his sad mood with a grim smile while we listened to the captivating music and stories.

As the evening wore on, the food bowls were replenished several times. Finally, Cristal resumed her attempt to help us understand what we were involved in.

"It is our hope," she said, "to use the Esseen crystals to reverse the magnetic poles of the planet and cause an ice age, which will eliminate the beasts of land, sea, and air. These creatures keep us from turning Atlantis into a garden planet, a paradise like our beloved Lamoria."

Even in light of everything these extraordinary people had told us about their fantastic origin and journey across the universe and the abilities and powers of their magical crystals, this explanation of how they intended to reverse the poles of the planet sounded absurd. Zoe and I looked at each other in disbelief. Whatever they were doing with their crystals, it had caused our nightmare—and who knows what else? Finding these noble people and their pristine way of life was a staggering contrast to all we had endured since our arrival that night on the storm-swept beach. But our loss was too grave, and there could be no compensation.

Cristal asked for a lock of our hair so that we would be counted among the first humans and listed as such on the Scroll of the One called Me. We agreed to participate in this ritual. Shakti came over and took the required lock with a snip from a single blade.

"It's late now," Cristal said. "We should rest before going to the Great Hall in the morning. Any more questions you may still have will be answered by the elder, Adama, when we are together tomorrow in the pyramid."

Everything about these people was comforting, so we readily agreed to attend tomorrow's meeting.

After we thanked Cristal for her gracious hospitality, Shakti took us both by the arm. "I'll show you where you sleep tonight," she said, escorting us to the upper rooms, which were furnished with plush full-body sleeping pillows. Sensing our grief, she added, "Take heart, my brothers. Tomorrow is another day in the eternity of our Creator's plan." Then, smiling tenderly, she withdrew.

Before falling to sleep, Zoe said to me, "I believe everything Cristal told us. These *are* the first people on Earth. We're back in the beginning with them somehow. You know, this must be the real version of the Garden of Eden."

"It's as good a version as any," I said. "But somehow, it just doesn't seem important anymore."

Losing Dad was crushing our spirits like a millstone. Sleep was our only sanctuary.

We awoke the next morning recovered from fatigue, but our grief remained undiminished. Shakti and her mother served us a wonderful breakfast of their version of pancakes and fruit juice.

Afterward, Cristal said to us, "Our elders, Adama and Evana, are the wisest among us. We will go to the Great Hall to see them. I am sure you will find something in Adama's words. He will make a way for you. Everyone is gathering there now to meet you."

Ever since we had met these people, they had expressed nothing but love and compassion for us, but this was little consolation for the all-consuming grief that filled me and overflowed in Zoe.

As Cristal and Shakti started toward the door, Zoe and I followed. Soon we were walking on the boulevard toward the pyramid. As we went in silence, the bright memories of last night's dinner party obscured the black abyss that was never far away.

The pyramid was tall, at least ten stories high. It had a long row of steps that led halfway up the center to a triangular doorway, which resembled the opening that had let us into the mountain. Here, at its point of origin, the beam appeared to be golden, not red as when viewed from afar.

The women started to ascend, and we followed, a few steps behind.

Looking out across the enchanted hamlet, Zoe broke his silence. "They came here *how* long ago?"

"They must have been here for a while," I said. "This doesn't appear to be new construction."

"Right. I wonder how long it took to build this pyramid."

As we reached the entrance, we realized that the pyramid was bigger than it looked from below. Before entering, we paused again to take in the breathtaking view.

"One thing's for sure," Zoe said, waiting until I looked at him. "These people know how to do the Eden thing."

"Everyone is waiting," Shakti said. "We can go right in." The velvet tones of her voice brought us out of our spell and into hers.

She smiled and took our arms as we followed her mother into the Grand Chamber. Over the entranceway, etched into the stone, there was an inscription:

WE ARE ALL THE ONE CALLED ME

Below the inscription, there was a list of the names of the original Lamorians, and beneath that the names of those who, like us, had been brought here by the time spike caused by the experiment they were conducting. The names "Elias" and "Zoroaster" were the last two on the list.

When we entered the Grand Chamber, we were overcome by mixed feelings of well-being and terror. What was going on here was not at all clear. Our benevolent hosts were sitting assembled for—we knew not what. But across from them were fifty or more of what seemed to be prisoners, standing together in a penned-off section attended by burly guards.

Some of the prisoners looked like eighteenth-century pirates, while others were dressed like Arabs, Vikings, and Japanese World War II pilots. There were also American pilots and sailors from various periods. They all had troubled looks on their faces and were loudly voicing their discontent.

Guiding us past these people, Cristal bid us to sit with her and Shakti. We were confused, but relieved at not being put in with the prisoners.

Turning to Zoe, I said apprehensively, "I don't know about this. Those people are under heavy guard."

But Zoe was preoccupied with Shakti, their eyes locked in silent contact.

"Zoe," I insisted, "what do you think about those prisoners? What is this all about?"

Shakti answered, "Unlike yourselves, these people are reluctant to believe our sincere desire for their well-being. There are some among them who believe we are not what we claim to be, and they have incited others against us. But I am sure both of you will cooperate with Adama's plan."

Then she took her place next to her mother.

"What difference does it make?" Zoe said to me. "So what, if they sacrifice us up to some pagan deity? Whatever their plan is, it really doesn't matter to us, does it? Look at us! After all we've been through, if this is the end of the road, I'm ready to call it quits."

I remembered Dad's words to Rosario back at the fortress, when he said that ultimately we did not fear death, and that there are some things to which death is preferable.

"Yeah," I said, "I guess you're right. Sometimes it's better to pass on to what awaits us than prolong an unacceptable alternative. Whatever they're gonna do with us, I'm sure it'll be quick. They don't seem like the torturing type. Anyway, what choice do we have?"

Zoe nodded.

Across from where we were sitting was the source of the laser beam that had beckoned to us all along. Now I could see that it was not actually a laser beam at all, but rather a cylindrical chamber that contained what I can only describe as a golden force field. A column of sparkling golden light particles that extended all the way through the top of the pyramid appeared brightest in the center. A long flight of stone steps led to a doorway halfway up the column.

Shakti presented us to the elders. "I discovered them," she

said in Italian, "when they appeared inside the Great Golden Crater." Then, turning to us, she said, "Our elders were the attending doctor and nurse of the nursery section of the mother ship. They escaped the devastating meteor storm in the saucer that landed by the Wizard's Hat. Now they are the patriarch and matriarch of the first humans on this planet."

She gestured to us to take our seats in the middle of the semi-circle. Then the one called Adama got up and started to approach us. He was a tall, well-built man, who appeared to be in his fifties. As this patriarch of the human race came near, I felt a spinning sensation from the bizarre reality.

Looking at us directly in the eyes, he began, also in Italian, "That you are here is proof that we will survive these perilous times. We are sorry that we have involved you and the others in our problems." As he said this, he gestured toward the prisoners. "But we shall try to make the best of the situation. We knew that our attempt to temporarily shift the planet's magnetic poles would also create a time spike that would pierce the future. But if we did nothing, our race would *have* no future on this planet. As this phenomenon reached your age, you were drawn into the ripple in time, which is our here and now. It is our theory that as we wind down the experiment and restore the magnetic fields to their prior positions, you should return to your previous reality."

"Nonlo credi!" a voice shouted. It was one of the Japanese pilots, who was frantically telling us not to believe Adama. "They mean to dispose of us," he continued in Italian. "There

is no place for *us* in their perfect existence. They are aliens....
They are not like us!"

Oblivious to the pilot's outburst, Adama went on, "Our
experiment will conclude shortly. We have little time to gather
and exchange information."

"How is it possible," I asked, "that all of these different peo-
ples can speak and understand Italian?"

He smiled. "What you are hearing as Italian," he said, "is
actually the sound of understanding. The power of the crystals
allows everyone to understand the essence of each other's communications."

What he said reminded me of the biblical story of the Tower
of Babel, in which people's ability to understand each other was
fragmented into many languages and dialects. I now realized that
we were in that place in time when everyone still understood
everyone else. Even in the face of all of this, we were feeling the
pain of our loss as we sat and listened to Adama. His explanation
sounded as fantastic as the experiment they were attempting. For
a moment, there was an awkward silence.

Then Zoe asked, "How long have you been here like this?"

"After a perilous journey," Adama replied, "and losing all
but our nursery section, we landed here some time ago."

Zoe let it go at that.

"Can you tell us," Adama asked, "what it was like to pass
through the time spike?"

I told him how we had discovered a submerged saucer, and
then I recounted the whole story that led up to this moment.

When I passed around our pictures of the saucer, they were astonished.

Zoe, whose attention was still locked on Shakti, took no notice of this commotion. But their mutual admiration was suddenly blocked by Adama, who positioned himself between them like a protective father.

When the chattering among his people subsided, Adama said, "What else can you tell us?"

Annoyed with the elder's obstructing stance, Zoe said with obvious impatience, "I can tell you this.... We've heard many legends about Atlantis. It was a great continent that sank from seismic upheavals caused by the Atlanteans' own technology. But few of my people believed that there really was such a place." Zoe paused as he stood up. "I can also tell you that the beasts of land, sea, and air belong to a time long, long before the time we come from. Our presence here can only mean that we have come back through time somehow. But when we first saw your spacecraft, it was under two hundred feet of ocean in an area we call the Bermuda Triangle..., which is well known for ships and planes disappearing there. Some people have a theory that sunken Atlantean crystals still cause ripples in time and space. Up until now, we were among those who thought that explanation was highly unlikely."

As Zoe spoke, Adama had the look of fresh understanding.

Then Zoe choked up as he continued, "Now we're here in this beautiful crater in the middle of a horrific reality. We've lost our father, and our lives have been ruined. I understand *your* plight.... I don't understand ours."

In our depression, it was impossible to apply their optimism to our hopeless situation. We had reached the end of our road and were giving up.

But then Shakti came over to Zoe, took his hand in hers, and said to him, "My dear brother, nothing is ever lost, and sorrow is a brief contrast to eternal joy. Remember, we are living raindrops falling to the sea. Upon arriving, we all return to the One called Me."

We heard her words and felt their meaning, but we were becoming despondent. Her poem, a variation of Themi's, was not doing it for us.

Zoe tried to explain. "I understand all life is one," he said, "but we are two individuals standing before you, mutated by time...and miserable."

He was getting that vacant look in his eyes again.

Adama said to him, "Take heart, Zoroaster, there is only good news."

His face was warm and welcoming as he waited for Zoe to look at him. When Zoe's eyes focused once more, Adama continued, "The good news is that nobody dies, everybody lives. Life goes on endlessly in an upward spiral. Everything in life is a metaphor for what we call the Great Mystery. You can describe it, you can embrace it, but you can never fully understand the Great Mystery. Sleep, for example, is our everyday metaphor for death..., and death is a metaphor for sleep. Just as you wake every new day refreshed from sleep, so does the soul awake

in a new day refreshed and ready for another round in an endless chain of lifetimes. The one thing we all share is the miracle
called Life. That is eternal. We are all the children of the Creator
of the Universe. We are here to become proficient in the expression of creativity. Even the most horrific days are nothing more
than harmless experiments that did not work out."

Although we heard Adama's message, our sense of loss and
grief remained.

Then another prisoner interjected, "Pretty words! But what
he means is that *we* are experiments that didn't work out, and
now they mean to send us back into the sleep called death!"

Once again, these words fell away unnoticed by Adama. I
didn't understand why they had no effect on me, but they didn't.
For some reason, I believed Adama.

"Your presence," Adama went on, "tells us that we succeeded
in establishing the human race on this planet. Seeing our ship
submerged is not surprising, considering the amount of time that
has elapsed. That ship cannot be destroyed by time or anything
else. It contains our crystals and all that is dear to us..., a time
capsule that can only be accessed by the One called Me. Our
experiment has provided us with a look ahead. We have added
your names to the Scroll of the One called Me. It is our desire
that you find your way back to where you came from. As this
experiment concludes, we believe you will return to your own
time and place. Go now with Shakti. Enter the Middle of the
Middle and rejoice in your inheritance."

He gestured up to the doorway at the top of the stairs, midway up the column of light.

As soon as he finished speaking, the prisoners were led up the steps under heavy guard. As they ascended to the entry of the chamber, they were screaming, reluctant to be cast into the golden force field. But their resistance was futile as each one was taken and thrown into the light.

Shakti then took us both by the hand and led us up the steps toward the center of the chamber, where the golden light was brightest. Unlike the prisoners, we offered no resistance. Whatever was going to happen next, we were ready to accept it. Our only hope was that the end was near.

Shakti led us further into the light. As we came to the center, it felt as if we were swimming through the intense golden beam. Then she released her tender grasp and was gone, lost in the light.

The golden particles illuminated every fiber of my being. They twinkled like a golden Milky Way, reminding me somehow of Christmas. The sparkling intensified until I recognized that the lights were a solid wall of golden fish. I looked at Zoe as we waited for them to pass, and then we both saw it beneath us. A hundred feet below, shimmering in the golden green light, a saucer was lying in two hundred feet of water.

Time was running out, so I snapped a couple of pictures, signaled Zoe, and we headed for the surface. When we came up, yelling about what we had found, we startled Dad. Seeing his expression as he watched the way we were swimming toward the boat, I could tell that he thought a shark was after us.

Postscript

Dr. David Abblett
Clinical Report on the Preceding Text
Subject: Elias Kazmir

Subject's brother, Zoroaster, is my patient seeking relief from new onset phobia, which made him unable to continue diving in their family business. Under hypnosis, Zoroaster related a fantastic chain of events, of which he had no conscious recollection afterwards. In an effort to get to the source of this problem, Elias also submitted to hypnosis and, over a series of sessions, gave a nearly identical account of the same events, recorded here verbatim. Like his brother, Elias had no conscious recollection of any of the events in this account that took place after they discovered and took pictures of a saucer-type craft lying in two hundred feet of ocean on the edge of an abyss off the coast of Bermuda. I have scheduled the next session with both brothers to present them with these findings.

FOREST FOX

Book 2

RENDEZVOUS
PIRATES OF MARAUDA TRILOGY

www.ingramcontent.com/pod-product-compliance
Lightning Source LLC
Chambersburg PA
CBHW031121030726
47496CB00002BA/627